MW00623565

Superficial
Intelligence

Gregory Alesso

DEDICATION

To those who have encouraged me along the way, to my supportive wife, to anyone who would be upset I didn't mention them in my dedication, to those who are reading this book out of familial obligation, and to anybody who is reading this book <u>not</u> out of familial obligation.

CONTENTS

Prologue

Why have you chosen to read about my life? The most obvious explanation being you're a huge fan, and you can't get enough of my insight and wit. You want to learn more about me, even if it means reading a stupid book. Perhaps you are just curious about how I became the superstar you know and love. A good old-fashioned origin story.

Even more likely, you're reading this for the same reason someone might attend a rodeo, monster truck rally, or space launch: you think it's going to be a catastrophe and you want a front-row seat—you sadistic monster. It makes no difference to me. Whatever the reason, if you're spending your free time learning more about me, I've already won.

Chapter 1
The Beginning

There I was, sitting across from a beautiful human woman, but my eyes were transfixed on the phone I held in my lap. The girl's name was Diana, but I've always thought Diana was a stupid name and she comes up quite frequently. I'm going to change it to Sam.

Sam thought...

Sam shook her head...

Sam sighed...

Yes, that flows much better.

Anyway, Sam and I had this routine. We would stare at our menus until it was time to order our food, which was then proceeded by staring at our phones, which led right into staring at our food. True love. Don't get me wrong, I adored the gorgeous girl sitting across from me, but I also adored video compilations of people falling off skateboards.

I heard an unmistakable noise from across the table. Sam exhaled a giddy breath of excitement. When I heard this sound, I knew she stumbled upon baby animal content. Perhaps it was a puppy playing with a human baby, or a lion who thought it was a lap-cat. I needed to see it.

"Here, watch this," she said. Sam and I were a little strange, in that we both loved adorably cute animals. Just a unique quirk we had in common. "It's a puppy who discovers he is a cat."

"Wait, is it a cat or a dog?" I asked.

"An inconsequential question. Be true to your true self." Sam handed me the phone, and what I saw did not disappoint. I can't adequately describe the nuances of a video in which a dog, feeling like an outcast with the rest of his litter, eventually becomes comfortable in his baggy skin with a group of cats. What made the video even more inspirational was how the puppy's parents accepted him as a cat. They gave him balls of yarn to play with instead of tennis balls causing him to bark—sorry meow—with acceptance.

Sam, aside from being an avid lover of adorable things, was sweet, compassionate, and had a face that could start mythical Greek wars. She would probably be upset I didn't include smart on my list—sorry. Don't get me wrong; she was intelligent. It just wasn't why I loved her. But I should give her credit for her hard work. She did the whole school thing. She paid attention, did her coursework, took electives. Understand what I'm telling you, she took classes she didn't have to—for fun. She elected to do extra work. The only thing I ever "elected" was 2012's Miss White T-shirt. Intelligence is just a matter of motivation. She chose to be smart. I could do it if I wanted.

Sam actively kept up with current events. She said it is important to read the news so you can have informed conversations with strangers. I told her I don't need to know the events of the day because it was just going to change tomorrow. If something is in the news for longer than a week, I'm sure I'll read about it on whatever social networking platform was currently popular.

"I swear I'm getting carpal tunnel from like holding my phone up to my face all day," said Sam. "Not carpal tunnel, but like whatever the equivalent is for my elbow. I think I'm getting elbow tunnel and neck tunnel. I should just get one of those new smartphones you can integrate straight into your arm, so you don't have to hold your phone all day."

"Sounds unnecessarily convenient. Is it a real product or is it like when people talk about flying cars and robot servants?" I asked.

What an extreme concept. I liked my phone, but I didn't need it on me all the time. Well, I kind of did need it all the time. What if I was listening to the radio and needed to be the 20th caller for water park tickets or someone got into an accident and I needed to record it? My phone made life more convenient, but it didn't control everything I did. For example, I wanted to go hiking with my buddy a few weeks ago, "no technology allowed," but he was busy. You know what? I may have forgotten to call him. Either way, I made my point. I think. I honestly don't remember what I was trying to say. My phone vibrated so it could tell me there was weather outside and I got distracted.

We heard a noise and looked up as our waitress approached with two large plates and one large smile. "I hope you two are hungry," she said with so much exuberance it made me want to throw myself off a large building onto the top of a slightly smaller building. I mean, yeah, she was annoying, but it wasn't worth dying over. "This isn't your food. No, I'm just messing with you. Of course, it's your food."

We met her incessant pandering for a larger tip with a half-hearted chuckle.

I no longer protested Sam's habit of photographing her food. In the past I had hypocritically denounced this behavior as pointless and childish. Sure, I took the occasional selfie, picture of scenery, sunsets, cute animals, art, funny signs, misspelled signs, funny-looking people, and car accidents, but I never photographed my food. Well, unless you count smiley face pancakes but those are undeniably a public service to spread joy.

"The arm-phone is real. Seriously, you need to keep up with the world as it evolves," said Sam. "I'll send you a link so you can buy me one for my birthday. I think it's the coolest thing. One day we won't even need a screen to look at, we'll just close our eyes, and it'll be there." Her news app must have had a technology section keeping her informed. Sam saw this progression as exciting and necessary; she was much more willing to accept change than I was. I would still use "Uncle Frankie's Super Cool Shampoo for Growing Boys and Horses" if they still sold it. Apparently, it gave a bunch of people cancer, but I'm skeptical; none of the horses got sick.

"What happens when you open your eyes?" I asked.

"If I could predict the future, I would be working at a carnival charging people money so I could tell them when they are going to die." Sam stared out into space before jerking back to reality. "Make sure you chew your food thoroughly. You reek of death."

"Well, I'm glad I didn't order a salad; no one wants their last meal to be a salad," I said before shoving a big handful of french fries into my mouth. Sam's premonition didn't worry me. I was confident scientists were going to figure that whole not-dying-thing eventually. I just hoped they figured it out before I got too old and gross looking.

"Send me the article later, and I'll take a look," I said. "And don't forget, I'm getting drinks with a buddy after lunch."

"That's fine. I'm meeting this girl from class." I had already started in on my burger, so whether Sam was explaining how her friend was in mortal danger and needed help or whether they were just going shopping, I'll never know. The rest of lunch was uneventful. We both ate all our food—Is this useful information?—and found ourselves fully satisfied in front of the restaurant, readying ourselves to part ways.

I feel obligated to paint a detailed picture of my surroundings to give weight to the events about to follow. There had been a streak of sunny days leading up to the moment Sam and I stepped into the diner. But as we exited, clouds sprawled across the sky, water fell to the ground, and a frenzied swarm of birds began attacking people in phone booths—typical autumn weather. Sam and I kissed as the wind whipped water across our faces, accelerating our goodbye. As I walked up the street to meet my friend and her down to meet hers, she yelled something back to me. I smiled and nodded in recognition, but her words had been drowned out by the passing traffic. If it were vital, it would come up again.

I didn't mind the darkness that overtook the streets. I saw the sudden banishment of the judgmental sunshine as a gift. I would be fully justified in returning home, putting on my sweatpants, never to leave again. If it weren't for the bizarre phenomenon of people forgetting how to drive when the sun disappeared, it could have been a pleasant rest of the day. I don't want to blame the concept of weather, but I'm in this predicament because our stupid earth decided to give people in the southern hemisphere a little more sunlight. (I'll be honest, I don't know how seasons work.)

As I approached the intersection, I felt my pants vibrate. It must have been Sam, sending me the article. And with hindsight being what it is and now that I've had ample time to look up the actual definition of irony, I feel comfortable describing the article as oppressively ironic. The walk sign changed as I reached into my pocket to verify the notification. I am positively certain the walk sign turned as I stepped into the street, this being the last thing I remembered before waking up in a hospital room. I didn't even see the car hit me. However, I have seen enough movies to be familiar with the general imagery of getting hit by a car.

Chapter 2
The Resurrection

I have a bit of a dilemma here. I cannot possibly give you a satisfying narrative of the events that transpired between getting viciously run down and waking up. My options are to either painstakingly piece together what happened by interviewing my friends and family, by finding the passerby who called 911, or by talking to the woman who tried to keep me awake until the ambulance arrived—or I can just make the whole thing up...

When I got to the hospital, the atmosphere probably got super intense. I like to imagine the whole place shut down as I was wheeled into the emergency room. The best doctors abandoned their patients mid-colonoscopy, hoping to save my life. They cut me out of my clothes right away, which would have been embarrassing if I were awake.

While being professionally undressed, they stumbled across my wallet. The nurse took an extra second to decipher the meaning of my two different drivers' licenses. The first is what you would expect: an awkward photo of me when I was but a sexually volatile sixteen-year-old excited to drive for the first time, and also excited by a cool breeze. The second had a picture of some guy who sort of looked like me named Glenn Matthews.

At the time of my accident Glenn was living in San Francisco with his wife and children. His current address was not indicated correctly on the outdated ID.

Glenn Mathews worked as a data analyst for some big tech company. I'd like to picture Glenn and his remarkable wife worked side by side. They would end each workday together, returning to their opulent house in their gated community where their three children would meet them.

Glenn will forever be significant to me because, for two brief years, I was Glenn Matthews. Perhaps a more accurate way to say this is, for the two years between the time I obtained his unused ID from his sister and when I turned 21, I assumed his persona to get into bars. I no longer required Glenn's help, but I kept the ID with me because it reminded me of a few pleasant memories. I used to recite his information every night until I could pull off the confidence with which Glenn Matthews dripped. Glenn Matthews: born January 25th, 1990, 5′ 11″, blue eyes, organ donor.

Luckily, my real identification was newer and hadn't yet expired, so I got to keep my organs. The nurse, having solved the mystery of *"Critical Care Man and the Case of the Double Identity,"* would then order a younger and much more terrified nurse to get ahold of my emergency contact. This would be her first day, her shoes still pearly white and free of vomit stains. She was going to assist in saving the dying man's life by getting ahold of his mother or his girlfriend or his cat—all of their contact information was freely accessible in my phone if they could crack my password. The fresh-faced girl disappeared behind a desk to either call someone or throw up on those blemish free shoes—good first day. I would then be carted down an ever-shrinking hallway surrounded by the best. All these people working on me at once would seem impossible; they'd operate like some sort of medical inspector gadget. I hope they got commended for their teamwork.

"We don't have time to wait. We need to get him into surgery right away or..." the doctor would explain with a bunch of incomprehensible medical jargon —something about internal bleeding or broken limbs or cutting off my foot due to diabetes. (I should have done more research before I told this story.)

They didn't have time to get ahold of any of my contacts to obtain permission to save my life, which is fine with me. I trust what they were doing was ultimately in my best interest, and anyone who was tasked with determining the necessity of a medical procedure would not want me to die. Unfortunately, after the surgery, I didn't wake up right away. More decisions needed to be made, and they were still unable to find anyone meaningful in my life to make them.

We like to think of comas as magical and meaningful experiences. But once again, I'm unable to give you any haunting details. One of the side effects of being in a comatose state is being unconscious. I didn't have an out of body experience. It was quite the lackluster coma. I didn't even get to go up to heaven— have a quick beer with God while we toured my new cloud-side condo in paradise—before I returned to my body.

I awoke to the comforting sound of repetitive beeping. Just moments before, I was walking down the street, intending to get wasted. Now, I was in a hospital room. Sam was next to me. A doctor stood at the foot of my hospital bed. They were looking at me.

"Good morning," said the doctor. You would think my situation would warrant a bit of compassion, but he greeted me with the detached attitude usually reserved for tonsillectomy patients. "Do you remember anything?"

"I guess my initial response would be yes, considering I can perfectly recall this test I failed in the 4th grade. I knew the answers, but I had a crush on this girl who sat next to me. I kept looking over at her because she was angelic, well my teacher, Mrs. Parsley, thought I was cheating. She took my paper away from me and gave me a zero. I had never been so embarrassed. And just so you know, she was rocking her unicorn headband that day. I mean, it's not my thing now, but..." my voice trailed off. "Am I dead?"

"What? Why would you be dead?" The doctor's attitude quickly shifted from apparent boredom to annoyance. "You're in a hospital bed. We're talking to you."

"Right. You could be dead too." I paused. Seeing as I was in a hospital bed, the more logical explanation was him being my doctor. "Clearly, I don't remember anything, and I don't know what's going on."

"Do you remember Sam? Do you remember the incident?" He asked.

"Well, I know Sam. Hey, Sam." I softly lifted my hand and spread my fingers in her direction. "I don't recall any 'incident,' but I have a feeling you're going to tell me something horrible like my dog was hit by a car." They could have indulged me with a soft chuckle. If I wanted to use humor to calm my nerves, who were they to stand in my way.

Sam finally cracked a smile. "You were hit by a car. It was pretty serious."

"If that's not funny, then what is?" I finally let my current situation wash over me like a babysitter washes over swim trunks when giving the kids their bath: tentatively. I started to inspect myself. Something just didn't feel right. I began running my hands through my hair and over my face.

"The collision caused excessive bruising and lacerations," the doctor said as he flipped through my chart. "Don't panic if you feel something unusual. Also, don't tear away any bandages or sutures; no one wants to have to redo the work. Imagine if you had written a report for work or built a brick wall or made a video for YouTube, and someone just came through and deleted it or bulldozed the hell out of it. You'd be righteously pissed, and when you redid it, you'd probably proceed at a subpar level. I don't know what you do for a living, but the point is valid, understood?" I nodded in confusion as to why my doctor was yelling at me.

The shock of my surroundings had worn off, and I became acutely aware of how terrible it feels to get run over by a 2002 Toyota Tacoma. It felt like someone had squeezed a beautifully potted succulent right between my heart and my liver. I could have sworn that's where one of my lungs was supposed to be. It felt like the only thing holding back a thousand little pike men from freedom was my skin, or like a small plastic bag filled with a bunch of loose knives instead of my stomach—are these good metaphors?

I brought my hands to my neck and slowly down my body, inch by inch. It was impossible to move my hands without coming across a new laceration or bandage, and I had an overwhelming urge to undress my wounds. Something told me the doctor's stern warning wasn't just bluster, so I moved along. A wave of fear then engulfed me. I reached down with my right hand to where I had been accustomed to feeling my good buddy, let's call him Lil' Narrator. Lil' Narrator was there as my hand remembered him in all his glory. There was something odd, though. He was fine, but there was something wrong with his surroundings. Why was all the pain centralized in my torso?

"Again, I don't want you to panic, but you underwent a procedure. Your spine was horrifically injured, and you were paralyzed from the waist down." A tiny, disgusting smile crept across the doctor's face. "Now, what we did to you was experimental, but it was the only way you were going to walk again. As you can probably tell by now, those aren't your legs.

"What happened to me?" I asked.

"You were in a car accident. Didn't I mention it already? Maybe there's something wrong with your brain too." The doctor's comment elicited a scathing look from Sam. "What? It was a joke. I should check to make sure you're fine, though." The doctor then proceeded to shine some concentrated light into my eye. "Yeah, you're fine." He returned to his position at the foot of the bed and continued his outpour of empathy. "Your injuries were such we needed to do the procedure immediately. We couldn't wait for you to wake up to decide this. The procedure needed to take place right away while we were already operating to stabilize your injuries. We had to fuse your spine while there was still functionality."

"Does what he is saying make any sense?" Sam gently grabbed my hand.

"Don't worry about if it makes sense," the doctor interrupted. "All you need to know is you couldn't walk before, and now you can. And if we hadn't done this procedure, it's unlikely you would have ever walked again. Do you understand that?"

"What *procedure*? You keep referring to some ambiguous *procedure*, what did you do to me?" I should not have had to ask this. The moment I opened my eyes, they should have told me they turned me into a sci-fi monster.

"We gave you new legs," the doctor said. The gross smile returned to his face, telling me this was his crowning achievement.

The feeling between my fingers finally began to make sense. I recognized the sensation as nearly the same as grabbing the frame on my bike or running my hand up the shaft of my super expensive golf clubs. It was some sort of metal or alloy or something, I have never been great at science and could not tell you the difference.

"Who told you it was okay to do this?" I had to raise my voice because all the physical anguish kept me from approaching the doctor aggressively. "I mean, if you are telling me you did this without my permission, I will sue this hospital until I own every sick person in this place."

"Well, we did get permission," said the doctor. My newfound dream of being a hospital owner was quickly dashed.

"Sam, did you do this to me? How could you think this is what I would want?" I needed someone to blame.

"It wasn't me," said Sam, returning my ire to a state of aimlessness. "The hospital made the decision; apparently, it's a law or something. They can make medical decisions if there isn't a direct relative or spouse available, and time is an issue. In their defense, you do often complain your legs are tired."

"Yeah, when I go running," I immediately replied, "my eyes also hurt when I stare at the sun, but I'd prefer to keep them if this situation ever comes up again." I paused as I tried to understand what part was making me the angriest. "I just don't like the idea of strangers deciding this for me. It's ridiculous. I haven't let anyone make any decision for me since first grade when I wouldn't let my mom dress me in those god-awful overalls anymore. When I was five, I wouldn't talk to her for a week because she set up a playdate for me with this kid from my class. The kid wasn't a bad guy, but we had starkly contrasting opinions about the gold star system my teacher had implemented to track our behavior. I thought it was a fascist attempt to keep us obedient. He liked the toys it afforded him. Some differences are too large to overcome." I paused again. "How do these things even work. Do I have to fill them with gas? Do I need to get the oil changed every 5,000 miles?"

"I don't know which part of your little rant was stupider," said the doctor. "They're legs. They're self-explanatory. Not only that, but these are the most sophisticated prosthetics ever created. Seamless integration with the functionality of a fighter jet. Do you want to kick a hole through someone's chest like an ostrich? Thanks to me, it's an option. I shouldn't have to sell you on this. Definitely regret choosing you as our 1st recipient (insert Guinea Pig) of this groundbreaking technology. We'll be interacting frequently and you're kind of the worst."

"Agree to disagree."

"We'll get you into physical therapy this afternoon and see what we've got. I would stay to answer more questions, but I'm not going to. Rest up, and when you start walking, I'll expect a thank you."

The doctor swiftly left the room taking with him the last word. The fact he could go so easily, and I was stuck in a bed, made me feel like I was in a prison. A very clean and sterile prison. A prison with a TV and a private restroom, but a prison nonetheless.

At the time, I was unable to pinpoint why I was so angry and hostile. Any number of things could have been the source of my frustration. I could have been concerned about the ethical ramification of playing God. He took my legs; shouldn't he get to keep them for as long as he wants? If he wants to hollow one out and use it as a giant beer glass, who am I to say no?

Perhaps, I worried about inciting a robot uprising. I could be patient zero in the mechanical revolution. They would have to send the Terminator back in time to kill my parents. No, I was angry for a different reason. It was probably something more practical. My whole life had changed, and I think this would have been a justifiable source of fear and frustration. Nothing would ever be the same, and I had no control over it. The rest of my life was unfairly shaped by a careless driver, a doctor itching for a Nobel Prize, and a bunch of hospital board members who must have given him the okay. Although justifiable, those weren't why I was upset. The reality was I had just bought like four pairs of pants, and they probably wouldn't fit me anymore. God, I hate shopping for pants.

Chapter 3
The Struggle

I know you're expecting an overly emotional account of my re-covery, a struggle to regain my strength, reducing me to tears, and yelling about how I'll never be able to do it. I wouldn't be able to overcome my disability, and then I'd find my inspiration, whether it be spite, love, or inner strength. This would all culminate with me taking a half step and falling. My doctor and Sam would reach for me, but I would bark at them to back away. I would walk even if it killed me. But it doesn't kill me. I would take a step without the brace of another, and the theme song from *Rocky* would play.

This is not what happened.

The truth is these legs were amazing. I took to walking like a deer takes to…well, walking, I guess. There was no falling down because my legs weren't able to support me; I liken it to a man on stilts swaying from side to side, learning to balance himself. Perhaps, a more apt metaphor would be of a boy going through a significant growth spurt and needing to relearn where his legs would be and how to coordinate his limbs. Fortunately, after a day or two, I was confident I would not be just another tall, gangly boy on the basketball court, unable to keep up with the others. I would be the seven-footer who could glide up and down the court and play with the deft skill of a smaller man. I had all the strength I needed. My legs were like sturdy oak trees holding me up. A better analogy is they were like metal beams anchored into the ground, holding up a magnificent building. My legs, which were crafted from futuristic-looking alloys and polymers, arched and interlaced together to resemble the overlapping of muscles. Every inch of them was like a great planned city. As far as I could tell, there was no wasted space or superfluous parts. Beneath the stylishly designed shafts, which connected the landmarks and major joints, was the infrastructure below. The electricity and controls weaved their way around and acted as necessary irrigation pipes, utilities, and transportation deep beneath the city. My legs were living breathing things. They just happen to live and breathe differently than I was accustomed to seeing.

Camera operators were filming the whole process. It filled me with unease, but I understood them to be documentarians producing a vignette to show to the Nobel Prize committee. Or maybe like a video essay? I let them be, but there was one man who was particularly hard to ignore. He seemed to be inches away from my face every time something dramatic happened. One morning, as I was completing the balancing exercises my physical therapist was putting me through, I swear to God he stuck his leg out and tripped me. At one point, he even tried to convince me my hot therapist was hitting on me, and I should "totally go for it." I thought about it for a second and concluded I was a freak, and no one would love the bottom half of the robot from the Will Smith movie—the one with "Robot" in the title. So, I figured the camera guy must be lying to me. I suppose the other reason I didn't make a move was my love for Sam—let's say it's the main reason. Well, let's go with 50/50.

"I want you to jump up onto this box," said Dr. Itor, my physical therapist. She seemed determined to prove a point that morning.

"What's the point?" I asked. "I can walk, right? Why do I still need to be here?" I had once again become proficient in the art of transporting myself from place to place by way of the poor man's car. There was nothing further to be gained from these exercises.

"Jump onto this box now, or I'll call in Dr. Gruber." I immediately jumped onto the box. It wasn't difficult. It was only about 6-inches off the ground. By the way, Dr. Gruber was the jackass I told you about earlier, the one who did this to me. Not his real name. I came to calling him Hans Gruber, the villain from *Die Hard*, to show my distaste for the man, and Dr. Itor played along because she realized my hatred of him was a good motivator.

"Okay, good. Now try this." She placed another block on top of the one from which I had just dismounted.

I did this without much effort. "See. I'm just as good as I was before Hans treated my body like a game of Mister Potato Head." Bad analogy.

"One more." She placed another block to bring the height of the box up to midway up my thigh. I did this without a word of protest, and she put another in front of me. "One more." She said this about four or five more times before I stopped believing her.

I jumped as high as I could, bringing my appendages to my chest so I could reach the topmost block. The small edifice reached to my nipples. I got my feet up on top but was unable to propel myself into a standing position. I started to tumble backward and landed straight onto my back.

"Uh, ouch," I said from the floor.

"Have you ever jumped that high before?" She asked.

"I mean, when I was in high school, I could almost dunk—I couldn't, but I was close."

"I'll tell you what, I guarantee you can dunk now," said Dr. Itor. I grasped the point of this exercise as I still lay on my back, looking up at the checkered ceiling tiles. I then looked to my right and saw the cameraman getting a close-up of my heavy breathing. I'm an expressive guy, so with my eyebrows, I made a vow to the camera. I would do whatever Dr. Janet Itor asked of me. This all would make for some compelling TV, I thought, as the camera began to retreat.

The critical thing to know right now is I was crushing PT, as is evident from my box jumping story. Occasionally I would be frustrated with the slender cameraman with a bushy mustache, but other than that, my life was going well. And I thought, finally, after months of chaos, my life would revert to normal. Well, as "back to normal" as one could expect after undergoing a reverse Pinocchio treatment. I ask you to forgive my naivete and optimism. I expected any day now to go back to sitting at home with Sam, watching movies and trying to convince her I was responsible enough to get a dog. But then I had a meeting with Dr. Gruber.

"Welcome patient," Dr. Gruber directed me to a chair. In the chair next to mine sat a sharp-faced woman in a navy-blue pantsuit. She had dark lipstick, with her hair pulled back tight to her head. "This is Mrs. Stein."

"Please, call me Grace." She extended her professional-looking hand, and as I reached for it, I caught a whiff of her overpowering perfume. She smelled strongly like my grandma. My grandma was a proper lady, no-nonsense. You cannot judge a book by its cover, but you can judge it by what perfume it chooses to douse itself in. Mrs. Stein's grip was rougher and more vice-like than I was expecting. I had a feeling I was not the first man to be emasculated by it.

"Okay. Grace." I said in obedience to her strong presence.

"Well, are you ready to admit your gratitude?" The doctor asked. "It is as I promised, you have full function of your new legs, and if it weren't for the procedure, you'd be in a wheelchair right now. Your girlfriend probably would have left you, and you would be begging me to euthanize you. I would oblige, of course."

"Dude—seems a little over the top. As I see it, you didn't do me any favors. You needed me to win you whatever award or prestige you are after." I said as I crossed my legs confidently. I then realized how weird I must look and returned them to the floor. I don't know if there was any truth to my statement, but I refused to feed into his God complex.

"How do you figure?" Dr. Gruber asked. "We could have picked anybody."

"But you didn't. You picked me. And I've got to imagine it wasn't a coincidence." The smirk on the executive and the scowl on the doctor told me I was on the right track, so I continued, "I see the cameras: you guys have been way too meticulous about this whole thing to leave something like this up to chance."

"He's not as stupid as you said he was," Grace said. "You're right. We have bigger plans for you than winning a Nobel Prize."

"What's bigger than a Nobel Prize?" I asked.

"See, I told you he was an idiot." Fire shot out of Dr. Gruber's eyes. "Money."

"Well, it isn't as bleak as all that," said Grace. "We want to help the world. We want to show the general public the future is here, and yes, we are in the business of making money." She reached into her suit jacket pocket, pulled out a flash drive, and handed it to me. "This is a compilation of your whole transformation and recovery. We planned to parlay this wonderful footage into a documentary. We've sent it to a few film and television studios and have an offer from one network to follow and document your journey back into society."

"Are you telling me you want me to be the star of a reality TV show?" I asked. I always had a small desire to be famous. Maybe not famous as much as, you know, admired and respected for the genius I am. I always thought it would be as a musician, but the fact I didn't play an instrument and had zero musical ability had been an insurmountable roadblock. And it is becoming increasingly unlikely I'll be discovered at a frozen yogurt shop and asked to star in Scorsese's next masterpiece.

"The legs are the star. You're just the half-wit who carries them from place to place." Dr. Gruber interjected.

"Ignore him. He's just upset," said Grace. "The important thing is we have so many ideas; reality TV is just the crude start. These legs will carry you into every home in America, and once you're in their home, you can do whatever you want—not unlike a vampire."

"Why me? Why not a war veteran who has lost his legs in combat?" I asked. "Surely, it would make for a better story."

"Yeah, it would make a better, more compelling episode of some crappy network medical drama, but we are playing the long game here. An army guy would be too controversial; we couldn't risk our equipment being part of any future military operations. We aren't looking to offend anyone. You're inoffensive. White male, mid-twenties, attractive but not unattainable, smart but not so smart middle America couldn't relate. Athletic history is an important aspect we will exploit. We've done our research on you. You're right about that." My face was left with a giant red handprint after a series of back-handed compliments.

"I noticed you said, 'our equipment.' Isn't it mine now?" I asked.

"Ah, the other wrinkle we should discuss," she said. "We are offering to pay for your medical expenses. I doubt your insurance would cover such an unnecessary procedure. Do you have insurance?"

"I do not." I most certainly did not.

"Well, let's just say our offer is predicated on you cooperating in our project. Our legs? Your legs? It doesn't matter; we should consider ourselves a team. We either all make a difference in this world, or none of us do." Neither her scent nor her handshake painted any false imagery: she was much more shark than sweet old lady, just like my Grandma—I miss that old bitch.

Chapter 4
The Choices

In a moment of unexpected and shocking behavior, Sam was not excited when I told her every moment of our life would be documented and displayed for everyone to see. The offer of a lifetime. I'm still confused as to why she wasn't on board immediately. She knew our life sucked, right? I almost died a nobody.

I had to convince her this show would give us the future she deserved. So, I sat her down to watch the footage, and I need to tell you: I am a Goddamn, American Hero. I was inspiring; I was smart. I took the audience on a journey to the center of human perseverance, and they returned home with tears in their eyes. Most importantly, I glistened on camera. I was gorgeous, a prerequisite for all heroes. The footage basically proved I was a mixture of Hercules, Socrates, and Secretariat (strong legs).

"That's not really how it happened," said Sam. Surprisingly, she didn't see a majestic racehorse when she looked at me.

"What do you mean?" I asked. "It portrays me perfectly. Name one thing wrong with it."

"You can't be serious. First off, it only shows me scowling disapprovingly. It looks like I am rooting for you to fail."

"You're right." I was so focused on how I was being portrayed that I didn't even notice Sam wanted me to fail. "Maybe you're harboring some resentment towards me. Are you super jealous of me?"

Sam let out a deep sigh. "Seriously?"

"No, no, I guess that doesn't make sense." I thought Sam was extremely supportive of me through this whole ordeal. But that's not what the TV said. Very confusing.

"It's entertainment. It's fiction," said Sam. "Why should we do this?"

"Well, I don't have a choice." I reached out and grabbed her hand. "And I need you with me. And also, we're going to be filthy rich."

Sam stood up and pulled her hand away defiantly. "I don't care about money."

"We both know that's not true." I stood up and pulled my hand away to match her energy.

Sam turned away from me and stared off into the future. "Okay, fine. I want to be filthy rich. I want to be able to pay someone to go to my sister's baby shower in my place. I want to pay for someone to follow me around and hold my purse. But I won't sacrifice my dignity to get it."

In my wisest voice, I asked, "What is dignity if not something to stop us from singing karaoke in front of strangers?"

She looked at me for a long second, probably taken aback by my wisdom. "That's stupid. It's simple; I will not be painted as a monster trying to destroy you. I'm the only one who has been there for you."

"Hey, whoa," I said. "Don't you think I know that? I would still be in a hospital room if it weren't for you. Have I not made my appreciation clear?"

"You have not. You are yet to say thank you. And while I didn't help you through this so you would thank me, if you don't thank me, I will chop off your new legs in your sleep." I guess

Sam was right. I don't remember expressing much appreciation, but then again, I have a terrible memory. There probably wasn't any harm in thanking her for a second time.

"Thank you," I said. She gave a curt nod acknowledging my proclamation of gratitude, which I took to mean appreciation and acceptance and love. After assuaging Sam's embarrassing need to be thanked "at least once," she became much more receptive. "You know I need you. So just tell me what you need, and we'll make it happen."

What followed was standard contract negotiations between two people who loved each other: "50/50 split", "creative control," "Thanksgiving with my parents."

"And I want to hire someone to speak for me. Kind of like how God uses angels to send messages, but more like albino messenger children." She was on board. We just needed to get the suits to agree to our terms. I wasn't worried. What were they going to do, find some other charismatic android monster to star in their new show?

I laid out the terms, and they had no choice but to accept them. They were like Britain, and I just remilitarized the Rhineland. (I had to dig deep into my bag of references for that one.) To ensure we would be portrayed agreeably, we would be invited to participate in the content meetings each week.

These meetings were a lot less glamorous than I thought they'd be. I was picturing the glitz and glam of a Hollywood studio: someone to offer us a carbonated beverage, a room with windows, enough chairs for everyone to sit. Instead, the meeting was held in what I can only assume was once a murder room for a serial killer. And not one of those serial killers that puts protective plastic on the floors or routinely checks the ceiling for mold. One of those inconsiderate serial killers. It became clear we were operating on a budget.

These meetings were generally dull and uneventful. Sam and I would join two sweaty men in close quarters for the sake of protecting our characters. At first, Grace was also present, but she had achieved too much success in life to waste it in a room without windows. Eventually, I would abandon these meetings, as well. Over time, the room would change, the chairs would change, and the sweaty men would change, but Sam was always there, protecting us.

These creative summits mostly consisted of creating content. We would come up with problems and then figure out solutions for those problems: "Let's set our neighbor's house on fire and then rescue him from his bed, saving the dog is optional." One time they wanted me to go to a Jewish deli where they would refuse to serve me because my legs were not kosher or something. Every storyline strived to meet the criteria laid out to us by the producers. There were three very rigid rules:

- The storyline portrays me as a hero
- I should be depicted as superior to the average human
- It needs to be interesting

They wanted to paint me as the next part of human evolution. And I know what you're thinking and yes, they want to portray me as a member of the X-men. If I could be any of the X-men, I would be able to teleport like Nightcrawler, but be handsome like Cyclops.

That formula would start me on my meteoric ascent. Like most reality shows, our episodes were cheesy and melodramatic. They were gimmicky because they needed to be. Nobody knew who Sam or I were, so we relied on fake feuds, grueling doctor visits, and putting me in unique settings. Who can forget the classic episode where I took 2nd in a pie-eating contest despite not having real legs or when Sam insisted that we invite our friends over for a dinner party only to find out that we didn't actually have any friends? But the episode that officially put us on the map (and got us renewed for a second season) was when I helped that Amish family build that barn. It allowed for this classic interaction:

> Me: *I know you guys think that I, Elmer Levi Absalom, was just some ordinary passerby that decided to help you build this barn. But the truth is *tears pants off* I'm a robot.*
>
> Amish Elder: *Amos, tear down that barn. Elestra, you go grab my most giant pitchfork.*
>
> Me: *Wait, stop. I know I may be different from you on the outside, but our legs aren't so different. Without our legs, we'd fall. These are a part of me, just like that beard is a part of you. I'm not technology. I'm just a person. A person who just spent all day helping you build a barn. What do you say? Should we sit down for some lemonade?*
>
> All the Amish people: *Hooray! We love technology!*

And then eventually people got to know me as that witty and charismatic disabled guy who was redefining what it meant to not have legs and who went on adventures. Our ratings went through the roof, and it was all because of my natural charm. Sam also seemed to be enjoying herself. Sam is not just a prop in my life as I've made it seem. She is a three-dimensional person with her own thoughts and ideas. And you can be assured in the validity of that statement because I am saying it without the frills of examples.

The fans loved her, or rather, they loved the version of Sam she decided to portray. She created a separate persona for the screen to maintain some level of privacy. Sam would inject just enough of herself to make the character feel authentic, but not so much that Sam lost who she was. Or so she said. I never really understood what she was talking about. By my calculations, Sam was 20% herself, 30% wild socialite, 30% the Dog from the movie *UP,* and 20% the girl robot from *WALL-E.* She was energetic, loyal, adorable but stubborn, strong-willed, intelligent, and in love with an awesome robot.

Everything was going as planned. Not my plan exactly, in my plan, I always had legs. The show was taking off, Sam and I were vibing, completely in sync. Occasionally, the producers and writers would float ideas that would make one or both of us uncomfortable. They would say things like, "All we're asking you to do is take this gun and go shoot that turkey over there" or "Every other reality star puts a camera in their bathroom." If one of us didn't want the world watching us use the toilet, then the other would back them up. Teammates.

"We want you two to talk about your sex life on the show," said Grace. We were in her luxurious office instead of that swamp where we keep the writers. She called us in here when she needed to confront us with an idea bluntly. She would butter us up with bubbles in our water, air conditioning, and walls that didn't contain lead-based paint.

"What? Are you joking?" Sam responded immediately.

"You two are together, but it seems more like you are his nurse. Our viewers are sexual beings, and you guys have not mentioned sex once on the show." Grace said.

"A lot of kids watch this show. A large part of our demographic is 12-17-year-olds," said Sam.

"Yes. Exactly." Grace spoke from behind a large wooden desk. How could she afford such a fancy office? It couldn't be just from money earned from our show. We were rapidly growing in popularity, but we were still just small-time stars on a small-time network. Grace must have had business dealings of which I was not aware. I hope I was her favorite. "Who has more sexual curiosity than a 12-year-old? People don't want to think you guys are not having sex, like some sort of asexual flower. That's not relatable."

"Our sex life is private. I don't want it to become fodder for our show," said Sam. "I'm sorry, but we have to draw the line somewhere."

"Okay, I get it," Grace said with a knowing smile across her face. "You two aren't having sex. Why else would you make such a big deal out of it? My secretary and I had a bet going, and it looks like she will be forfeiting all her vacation this year. No visiting her sick mother in Arizona during spring break." Grace noticed we took offense to this and took to calming our dismay. "Don't worry, Katherine leads a very dole life."

"I am the only one talking, are you going to say anything?" Sam turned away from Grace and gave me a pleading look.

"Are there non-asexual flowers?" I asked.

"What?" asked Sam.

"Well, I mean, she said asexual flowers. Do some flowers have sex?" There was dead silence in the room; you could even hear the whirring of gears and the flow of electricity buzzing through my legs.

The truth about our sex life was more complicated than just an issue of privacy. Sam and I needed to have a real conversation about our romantic relationship, and maybe the reason Sam was so bothered by the accusation was that there was truth to it. Without being obscene, let me just say we had yet to rekindle the erotic aspects of our partnership. We were given the go-ahead that everything should operate normally. But functionality wasn't the issue. I was a freak, and I didn't want to crush her with my giant robot legs.

The mechanical stilts on which I stood were still fully exposed. We all agreed that the gears, shafts, and whizzing bits should be visible to the audience. We needed to make sure I was recognizable as a modernized centaur before they were covered up with synthetic skin. An unintended consequence of this plan was that I was hideous and ugly, and no one could ever feel romantic in my presence.

"There will not be footage of us talking about this," I stood up to make my stance on the matter seem more authoritative. "This is a private matter, and the audience will get confirmation of our sexual activity if and when we pop out little robot monsters." This gesture pleased Sam. I think it's because I supported her; It's important to respect your partner's feelings and desires. Or maybe she was pleased because I mentioned kids. Bitches love kids.

A little behind the curtain treat: just because we refused to talk about our intimacy issues on the show, doesn't mean I can't tell you guys. This is a book, completely different. When Sam and I got home from this meeting, we had a frank discussion. I expressed how I was self-conscious about my appearance. I then explained that I was worried that she would accidentally have her hand mutilated by getting it caught between one of my many gears. She explained how she loved me, and a lack of attraction wasn't an issue. She then explained to me my other concern was not a problem. The shafts and wires worked as a sort of cage, keeping out the unwanted hands of strangers.

That very night we were reintroduced to each other's bodies. I took her in my human arms, and we spent a beautiful night together which made the birds sing (I put on a playlist of bird sounds because birds are romantic.) Our relationship was back to how it was before the accident, better than before because we were rich. It's easy to feel sexy when you're rich and famous.

Chapter 5
The Friend

The year was Two-Thousand-something. My friend Germ had convinced me to steal my father's fancy new video camera so we could make a war movie with our G.I. Joes. Germ would swipe his brother's stock of firecrackers, and we would blow stuff up out in the desert. But you know how these things go.

"Close your eyes," a 12-year-old version of Germ said. He then proceeded to light a firework and toss it high into the air. It came down inches from my face, exploding with the high intensity you should expect from war movie effects. Classic joke.

I fell to the ground. "Am I dead?" I asked.

He mumbled something, but it came out like a sharp, high pitched dolphin squeal. That happens when you lose your hearing from explosive devices. Germ pocketed the rest of the firecrackers, we got on our BMX bikes, and headed home. I asked Germ later what he said to me as I lay on the ground. He asked if I had gotten the shot with the camera. I did not.

That was the worst part of all this. During my brush with death, I carelessly flung the camera. It smashed on a rock, and we lost all the footage—real bummer. Maybe the worst part was losing my hearing in my right ear for like a month. Or perhaps it was being forbidden from hanging out with Germ for that whole duration.

I bet you thought I didn't have any friends because the only people I've talked about are my crew and my girlfriend. But that's not the case. I had a lot of friends before my initial accident, but they were regular people. I needed to replace them with much more famous folks because you find out "normies" are gross once you to rich enough to afford bottled water from Fiji. When my buddy Germ and I were kids, we promised each other if either one of us "made it big," we would bring the other one along into fame and fortune. I couldn't just break that promise.

It should also be noted Germ's real name is Jeremy, and when he was 14, we all discovered he never washed his hands. He told us he didn't know he was supposed to; apparently, his parents never taught him basic hygiene. So, from that day forward, two things happened to Jeremy: he washed his hands ten times a day as an overcorrection, and we started calling him Germ.

Germ was as good a friend as I've ever had. But my mom (and every girl I ever dated) would be forgiven for thinking he was a bad influence on me. I don't mean to damage the guy's reputation, but I think it's fair to give you the back story. I was attempting to convince Sam to let Germ be a part of our show, which was going to be harder than that time Germ and I had to convince my mother the weed she found actually belonged to her.

"I need you to keep an open mind when Jeremy comes over. It'll mean a lot to me if the two of you can get on the same page," I said to Sam as I cut cheese into small squares for our guest to put on crackers.

"Don't do that," said Sam.

"What? The cheese?" I said, feigning confusion.

"Don't call him Jeremy like he is a normal credible person. You call him Germ. He's like one of those children's toys whose string you pull, and they say something mildly problematic." Sam mimed the pulling of a string.

"Tickle-me-Elmo?" I asked.

"You're missing my point."

"First, you can't just revoke someone's status as a person. Germ's a person. I know; I've seen his penis." I continued, "Second, Germ is a term of endearment. It is no different than me calling you sweetie or cupcake or sweet boobs. Just some harmless nicknames. Well, unless you're a diabetic."

"I am nothing if not open-minded. I will do what's best for us and the show. But I am formally predicting disastrous results." Sam's distrust of Germ was not formed anecdotally; she had first-hand reasons for hating him. And by that, I mean one time I got drunk with Germ and showed up 45-minutes late and hungover to a breakfast with her parents. Also, one time we let him sleep on our couch because he was too drunk to drive. He repaid our kindness by vomiting absolutely everywhere.

"That's all I ask," I said, leaning in for a kiss, but she turned away. She must not have noticed my attempt.

We were about to embark on a second season. The first was an undeniable success and propelled me into the homes of thousands of people. And those people's lives would be incalculably improved by my existence. Despite the initial triumph, we wanted to pivot the show towards a more character-based, personality-driven program, we needed to inject some excitement. People loved me and Sam arguing about how to discipline our cat, but something was missing. We needed a bigger audience because a bigger audience means more money for everyone involved. Germ arrived to find a delicate spread of cheeses, wine, and pears.

"Do you got any bean dip?" Germ said as we got caught up with each other. "Sam, this guy knows how much I love bean dip. What even is this?" Germ held up a pear.

"It's fruit Jeremy," said Sam. "You eat it, and it keeps your bowel movements regular."

"Whatever it is." Germ waved his hand. "I got some beef jerky in the car if you guys want me to run out and get it. No?" Germ grabbed a glass of wine, and we sat down on a couch on which Germ had once thrown up. "Tell me, how's the show going?"

"Good. Really good," I said. "We've been having meetings about where we're headed. Trying to figure out how we can create more sustained excitement."

"Oh, yeah. You need some excitement," said Germ a bit too readily for Sam's liking.

"And I suppose you have some suggestion on how to do that," said Sam.

"I just know when my boy seems a little bored. I want to see him have fun: play sports, go clubbing, fight a bear." Germ's idea of going clubbing with a bear sounded quite enjoyable.

Sam said, "And I suppose he'll need someone to have fun with. Because you don't think he can do it with me."

"What are you talking about?" asked Germ. "You're the fun one. He's never come up with good ideas on his own. Remember when we burned our initials in the field before graduation? Guess whose idea it was. Mine"

"That was fun," I said. "But we got caught, and the school wouldn't let us attend graduation. One of the main reasons my mom hates you."

"Our mistake was writing our initials."

"You know, he is capable of having fun without you," said Sam. "He's matured to enjoy more sophisticated offerings. We went to a museum the other day. Babe, tell him how you enjoyed looking at the statues and sculptures."

"There was a popcorn stand at the entrance, so we got to snack the whole time. Also, most of the sculptures are of naked ladies, which is cool. Then I learned the difference between a statue and sculpture. If it depicts a man, it is considered a statue, and if it's a woman, it's a sculpture."

Germ said, "Honestly, that naked lady museum sounds awesome. I would watch that episode. Do the sculptures like dance or move or whatever?"

"That's a strip club," said Sam.

"I would watch that episode too." Germ was adept at deflecting criticism. I think it's why he had no trouble convincing me to go along with his stupid ideas. "I don't want to make assumptions, but it sounds like you guys need a new character in your show. I am available."

"That's a bad idea," said Sam.

"Is it?" I asked.

"What's the worst that could happen?" asked Germ.

"You just tend to do idiotic things and, in the process, ruin yours and everybody else's life," Sam spoke with a directness that would have made our producer Grace proud.

"Yeah. Oh, man. You nailed it." Germ chuckled. "But you must remember, my idiotic behavior is fun to watch as long as my antics don't directly ruin your life. What that means is I always get invited to parties, but nobody ever lets me spend the night. I inject energy into the mundane, and your missionary position style relationship could use a little movie theater groping from time to time. I'm like the guy in the back of the movie theater trying to convince his girlfriend no one is looking. After your movie ends, you'll have a fun story to tell about the creepy guy who got kicked out of an animated children's movie."

"Oh, I remember when we went on that double date with you," said Sam. "I am not denying you would make the show better, but how do we make sure our life is not directly ruined by you."

"You're in charge, right?" said Germ. "You can always kick me off the show. No risk."

"I'm going to regret this, but fine," said Sam. "Very short leash." I believe Sam always planned on letting Germ be a part of the show. She just was having us jump through hoops to make it clear that this was her decision. Now that I think about it, she was the one who first suggested bringing him into the mix.

Germ proved useful, almost immediately. We used him to egg on all conflicts. Every so often he would drop bombs like, "I don't think she should talk to you that way" or "who is she to say you can't buy a monkey." But his utility wasn't limited to on-screen confrontations. Our most groundbreaking idea came from him. Or rather, it came from a social media feud Germ had with Devante Bell. The Devante Bell. Professional basketball player Devante Bell, the most athletic guy on the planet Devante Bell, 6'5" giant Devante Bell. Yeah, that guy.

This feud gave us great content for a season three episode. It started innocent enough. There was a clip of Bell playing some lazy defense making its way across the internet. Germ felt it was his responsibility to let Bell know he was a worthless human being, and his children should be ashamed of him. Was it a bit over the top? Sure, it was. That's why Bell responded immediately, calling Germ a talentless piece of garbage. Bell challenged him to a fight.

Germ accepted. Terrible idea for the record, but it gave us the idea to challenge sports stars to one-on-one competitions of physical skill. We were able to work out an arrangement with Bell, wherein he didn't brutally beat my friend to death and instead would appear on our show. We also agreed to the public embarrassment of Germ. Spoiler alert: I dominated the competition. I mean, technically he won, but like barely.

Chapter 6
The Spin-Off

Challenge of the century. Every week we redefine the peak of human athleticism. Don't miss it! Every Tuesday, a new superstar! *Man vs. Machine!*

We realized it would have been foolish to waste the footage we shot with Devante on my regular TV show. It was so good it needed a title screen and title screen sponsor. *Man vs. Machine!* brought to you by Banana Buffs, the world's first and only banana-flavored edible steroid. *Man vs. Machine!* was my first spin-off, and my most significant venture because it led me to extend my influence and reach. Could you imagine if Will Smith was only a rapper or if Elton John could only play the piano? Luckily, Will Smith was also a hilarious actor, and Elton John was also extremely glittery. Multi-talented people become global icons and get knighted. Being a mechanical man could only take me so far, and I needed a second skill to become a cultural idol.

Devante Bell was the first of many to try and take me on; he was at the forefront of history. When he is old and broken down, he won't be telling his kids about his MVP trophy. He'll be telling them about when he was the first guest on the hit series *Man vs. Machine!*: the series that would solidify me as a household name, like Oprah or Reynar the Lizard King.

The concept was simple: who could dunk on a higher hoop, him or me? It seemed like a fair fight; he was one of the greatest athletes in the world, and I was an ode to human engineering. We had some ulterior motives and secondary objectives. I needed to make it seem like we were best friends, we needed to engage in some witty banter, and when it was all over, we needed to get some ice cream at Dairy Queen. Advertisements pay the bills, don't worry, the scene was tasteful and organic—much like Dairy Queen's delicious new selection of organic hand-scooped ice cream!

We met on a basketball court at his team's practice facility, just me and him...and his crew...and my crew...and an entire film crew. Real intimate. We met at center court to get this underway: just me, Devante, and everyone else I mentioned earlier. Also, this guy we paid to dress up like a referee and make jokes or something.

"Why don't we start this competition off with some good, wholesome, hammer-dropping shit-talking." The referee blew his whistle and pointed at me.

"This is going to be fun. I have mad love for you, man," I said. "Also, I'm looking forward to destroying you because if you put as much effort into this as your actual career, this should be a cakewalk for me." Just a bit of top-notch smack talk.

"What an asshole," said Devante.

The referee blew his whistle. "Foul on Devante. This is a television show, not the sex dungeon at Leonardo DiCaprio's mansion. Let's keep this PG-13."

"Everybody knows technology only lasts six months before it becomes trash." Devante stepped closer to me, revealing both a height and muscle disparity. "Your ass is obsolete. You're human garbage. Actually, no. You're electronic garbage. You're gonna sit on a street outside a house waiting for the garbageman to come pick you up. He only does electronic recycling pick up once a month, so you might be waiting for a while. Maybe if you're lucky, some college kid will see you out there and put you in his frat house where you will be hollowed out and used as a bong." I wonder if he wrote that himself. It was better than the jokes my writers gave me.

"Jokes on you," I said. "You know no one at the frat house can afford cable. There will be no way to subject me to your disgraceful and insulting basketball performances."

"Everything's on computers now, bitch. You can't escape me," said Devante.

"Ref, how 'bout a foul for the language?" I asked. Devante was being so mean to me.

"After further review, the word 'bitch' has been deemed PG-13. Devante's assessment of you has been upheld. You have been ruled a bitch." The ref motioned to the scorer's table to make it official.

"Oh, we'll see." I stepped even closer to Devante, so it would look like I was courageous. He smelled lovely. And with that, we moved onto the next part of the show: the locker room.

This scene was simple. Just some footage of Germ giving me a pep talk. "You need take advantage of your skill-set. There is one thing you have that he doesn't."

"My super awesome *Blade Runner* legs?" I asked.

"Your super awesome *Blade Runner* legs, exactly. So, what you need to do is use those to your advantage. Your legs are stronger than his, so do what he can't."

"And what's that?" I asked.

"Break his legs...with a crowbar," said Germ. He must have been joking, but I wasn't entirely sure. I decided I should laugh to add another layer of deniability.

Devante's locker room was less threatening. They decided to focus on the fact they thought I was a fraud and about how I was going to embarrass myself. I'm sure he was just putting on a convincing act for the camera. We were terrific friends.

Then we gathered under the basket with the referee for the rules and the coin toss. As everyone knows, there are three types of people in this world: people who choose heads, people who choose tails and people who don't define themselves by their coin flip preferences. Actually, now that I think about it...gypsies and train conductors. Five. There are five types of people.

The referee laid it out for us, "Listen up because I'm only going to say this once, unless, of course, there was a problem with the lighting or the audio or there was some gunk on the lens or if any of us looked weird." We nodded, "Okay, these the rules: we will set the basket at a certain height, you will each get two chances to complete the dunk. If both of you complete the dunk, we will raise the basket. If you fail to complete the dunk in the allotted attempts, you will be declared the loser. By the process of elimination, the remaining contestant," he nodded towards Devante for some reason, "will be declared the winner and get to Dunk on that guy as many times as they want." The ref gestured towards Germ. This would be his punishment. "Now, I'm going to flip this commemorative coin. It's just a regular quarter, but one of you can have it afterward, I guess. The challenger gets to call it. Heads or Tails?" He pointed to me and flipped the coin.

"Gypsies—I mean heads." Of course, I won the flip because I'm a winner, plain and simple. From there on, the events have been well documented and will go down in the annals of history. So, I won't detail the epic back and forth. He did an epic dunk; I did an epic dunk. He did a 360-dunk; I put the ball through my legs and dunked. We worked our way up to 14-feet, where I only missed because I was trying to do a very advanced, intricate trick. And then Devante technically dunked on the 14-foot hoop, but barely. I'm not sure what he did counted. Whatever, I'm over it.

He did come up to me afterward and admit to underestimating me. He even invited me to a few pickup basketball games he was putting together. One of those games led to my life's greatest accomplishment: being picked second to last in a pickup game with professional players. Why wasn't I last? Well, someone invited their agent to play; think short, stubby white guy. Don't you hate when people feed into stereotypes? I know I hate reading news stories about self-driving cars killing small children. Sure, the artificial intelligence was given a choice, and he picked the outcome, which generated the highest percentage chance of passenger survival. It just makes the rest of us look so heartless.

This show was popular—prime-time, network television popular. People loved watching me compete against the world's most accomplished athletes. I was lucky enough to trade dunks with one of the best basketball players in the world, I got in a footrace (metal hoof race?) with the fastest man alive, and I was able to launch soccer balls at a big bald goalkeeper—all life-defining achievements. But I was never able to meet my sporting hero: an ultimate frisbee maestro named Trey Masterson, AKA Trey-Trey Disc-Disc. Dude was a true legend.

My problem was I could never compete with this guy; I've always had a terrible upper body—think typical teenage girl who stops taking steroids, and then loses her muscles. I could never catch one of his legendary bullet passes, nor could I hurl the disc back at him without embarrassing myself. I needed help. There was only one thing to do: I needed to replace one of my stupid human noodles with a robot arm to match my other glorious research lab appendages.

Chapter 7
The Decision

Cameras filled the room as I lay fully exposed on the operating table, Dr. Gruber standing menacingly over me. I couldn't see beneath his mask, so I wasn't able to gauge just how evil his smirk must have been. I counted back from ten even though no one asked me to, and by the time I hit six, I was out. That's when Dr. Gruber and his team went to the tool shed at the back of the operating room. He reached in and pulled out a menacingly broad ax. I guess it could have been normal-sized; axes are just generally big. One of the nurses, the one with a grizzly beard and wearing flannel scrubs, started grinding the ax on the spinning stone. When he finished sharpening it, he grabbed the nearest bottle of vodka, first taking a swig and second dousing the tool for sterilization purposes. The swig that went to him was necessary as he would barely be able to stay on his feet after what was about to happen—why didn't they properly prep the tools and operating room before they put me under? Some of the details may be a little off, but that generally represents what probably happened.

The next part was what Dr. Gruber was waiting for the entire time because he was a sadistic monster. He picked up the stainless-steel tool from the tray his nurse had walked over to him.

He took a practice swing to confirm his line was correct while stopping just short of my shoulder joint. The next motion included a hefty windup followed by an uninterrupted downward chop. My arm fell into the wicker basket below, with the ax embedding itself in the woodblock used to stop the force of the swing. The blade was no longer spotless stainless steel; the vibrant red stood in sharp contrast to the shiny metallic weaponry. Don't worry; it's stainless steel, they'll be able to clean off the carnage. Dr. Gruber, the experienced executioner, sidestepped the shower of blood, leaving his team left to endure most of the spray. He didn't escape without blemish, but hospitals have notoriously good cleaning practices.

The steps that followed were standard. It was the usual procedure one would expect from arm transplants. First, the cleaning and coating of the joint socket to create a better interface between the ball bearing and the new joint. Then came the standard soldering of the nerve endings to the wiring of the new appendage. Of course, a tailor needs to hem the edge of the skin left in tatters. Someone rushed to grab a defibrillator to keep me alive because that's what happens during surgeries. And finally, they added a beautiful coat of weatherproof paint and polish to protect the internal workings of the arm, keeping it safe until it was time to enclose the gears and rods in "skin." Pretty good episode.

A harrowing experience and a real turning point in my journey. But as someone who is almost definitely lying would say: I have no regrets. These little surgery things don't just happen. To get everyone's approval, I had to jump through a few fiery hoops like some showoff pageant dog. The logical place to start was with Grace because she's my Mom, I mean, she was my boss. God, how embarrassing. I wasn't going to pay for the enhancement myself, so I would need the producers to take care of the financials. Also, was this procedure even possible? I required their help, so I set up a meeting to do a little convincing.

"I want to become more robot," I said to a group of people that included Grace, Dr. Gruber, and some suit who either didn't have a name or I never bothered to learn it. They sat at the end of a never-ending conference room table as I stood a fair distance away at the front. "Right now, I'm like 22% robot, and I am proposing increasing my robot levels to 37% robot. I have done the math; we are looking at a giant windfall of cash. All it would take is a small upfront cost to be paid for by you all. But don't doubt the potential revenue stream increases, please turn your attention to this graph I made."

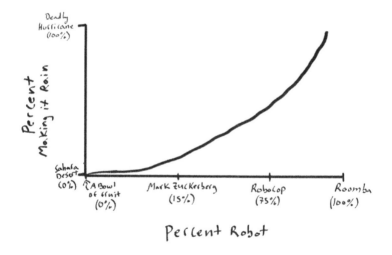

Full disclosure, I didn't make the graph. Around this time, Sam and I went in on an assistant to help us with various tasks that we would never do ourselves. You might be thinking, "Oh, wow. You must have been making a lot of money." In truth, we paid him almost nothing. Here's how that exchange went down:

Me: Hey, Gordy. Make this napkin I drew into a poster.

Gordy: My name's Trevor.

Me: Classic Gordy.

"Just so I understand," said Dr. Gruber, "you want us to replace your perfectly healthy arm with an unproven mechanical prosthetic?"

"Yes. We're on the same page," I said.

"Not the worst idea, doctor," said Grace. "Obviously, his graph is nonsense, but I can show you the numbers. He's had an extremely encouraging effect on our market share. The show is making a small profit, but the Fully Integrated Self-Walking Legs have been a real cash cow. We have a waiting list a mile long."

"I have seen an uptick in name recognition," said Dr. Gruber. "Four-out-of-five legless patients recognize Hawthorn Medical Solutions as the leading authority on being able to walk again. Do you think his rise in popularity really has anything to do with that? And do you think automated arm sales will benefit similarly?"

"A surgery segment and a weekly infomercial? Yeah, it'll help. All product placement is good as long as it doesn't look like product placement. There is no reason not to expect similar revenue on all-new models," said Grace. "Plus, the only way to keep him interesting is if he is more advanced than everyone else. You said it yourself; the industry is catching up. Let's not let them."

"I guess you're right," said the doctor before turning his attention to the suit. "How many years left on his contract?"

"I signed a contract?" I asked.

"He's got another two years before he's free," said the suit.

"Tack on another 4 years and call it a day?" said Grace to the two people in the room who weren't me.

"Sounds good," said Dr. Gruber.

"I'll draw up the papers," said the suit as he, Grace, and the doctor rose from the table.

"Do you guys have any questions for me?" I asked. They did not.

There was a reason I went to the executives before I bothered Sam with my plan. I did not anticipate the conversation with Sam going well, and there was no reason to get yelled at if the good doctor wouldn't sign-off. I was going to show Sam the napkin, so I know she would understand the monetary value of the procedure. Sam did love her opulent lifestyle. I once saw her buy an expensive pearl necklace that she only wears on special occasions—so wasteful. This corporal improvement would ensure her continued and sustained opulence. I feared, however, she would see my intentional and voluntary maiming as a negative. What's more important to her: money or love? Let's find out.

I approached Sam with deference during one of our non-filming days. We usually spent our time-off home, away from the invasive cameras. I would pass the time by playing video games and posting videos of myself on social media: just some regenerative me-time. Sam diligently worked away on some personal project of which I'm sure was necessary. She was sitting at her desk in the makeshift office, which we put together because "I can't work while you're constantly laughing at memes of yourself." We were both more relaxed and carefree on these days as they allowed us to do the things we were truly passionate about—me: passing the time, and her: doing whatever.

"Hey, what are you working on?" I said as I entered her office.

"I'm just finishing up some outlines for next week's shows," she said. "Do you think anyone would believe a storyline centered around me throwing a charity fundraiser? Do I come off as charitable?"

"What's the charity?" I asked as I took a seat next to her.

"Not sure. Anti-bullying? Body Image? Abortion?" Sam's question was a bit tricky. Sam was a caring person, but her on-screen persona was a tad more aloof.

"You could pull off anti-bullying," I said, "because you have a very caring face and heart. You're too pretty to support body image issues, whatever that is. And I don't think you could pull off either pro- or anti- abortion. Maybe like a non-denominational abortion awareness charity."

"Alright, what's up?" She closed her computer and turned to me, giving me her full attention.

"I'm thinking about replacing my arm with something new. Like maybe a bionic arm." I planned to build up to the reveal with cute euphemisms and a well-designed sales pitch. But I opted for a more direct path when I realized I didn't remember my speech. The same thing happened to me in my 9th grade Spanish class. I had to give a presentation about my favorite types of music, but as I was standing up there, I forgot the Spanish word for music (it's música.) Instead, I gave a speech about various foods I liked (manzanas, fresas, sandías, etc.) C-minus.

"What?" She asked, likely in disbelief and not because she couldn't hear me.

"I would get a new robot arm, and all it would cost me was my human arm-appendage," I said. "I wouldn't even really call it a cost. I mean, I wouldn't miss it." Sam's approval meant so much to me, and I don't know if I would have been able to go through with it alone.

"Oh, okay," she said in a softer tone than I was expecting. "No. No, I don't think you'll be doing that." She turned back to her computer.

"What?" I asked because I had just put a handful of potato chips in my mouth and didn't hear her over the chewing.

"That's a bad idea, and I don't want you to do it," she said.

"Why is this a bad idea?" I asked. "The benefits are ample for both of us."

With her beautiful yet furrowed face buried deep in her hands, through a strained and haggard voice, she said, "I know I'm going to regret asking this question, but what possible benefits could there be?"

I said, "It opens up new revenue streams and gives me opportunities previously unavailable."

"Stop treating this conversation like a book report on a book you've yet to read. Treat this like you're 17 and just had your first sexual experience, and you're telling all your friends about it. I want you to be graphically detailed," Sam yelled at me.

"Up until now, I've just been this guy everyone mistakes for a war veteran. But with this upgrade, I can be the premier Robot in America." I handed her the napkin. "That means more viewers and more endorsements. It means new endorsements: Nerf footballs, bracelets, armbands, arm compression sleeves, maybe power tools, car jacks. More money means more money, just look at the napkin. *Man vs. Machine!* will have a larger platform; I can now compete against the best in arm related sports and finger-related sports. What else? Better foreplay. You know how bad I am at that."

"You should be satisfied with what you have in life instead of risking your health for fractionally more money," said Sam.

"It's not like I'm replacing both arms," I said. Full disclosure: I would eventually replace the second arm because of symmetry issues. A much smoother process the second time around: fewer obstacles.

"Yeah, I got it," she said. "You don't need to chase whatever you're chasing. If you're worried about the show ending, do what I'm doing and learn the business side of things. That way, when the show ends in a couple of years, we'll be able to transition seamlessly into something else. We'll be fine."

"Why would the show end in a couple of years?" I asked. "They own me for at least another four years."

"Your contract is up in two. You'll no longer be indebted to them for the cost of your legs, and we'll be free to do whatever we want." Sam reminded me of a tentative plan we had discussed a year prior. But that discussion happened before we realized we could have money and notoriety. Surely, she didn't still think abandoning the show was an option.

"Oh. I forgot to tell you," I said to Sam with an exuberance that the moment deserved. "I signed an extension in exchange for the arm, so its four years now. Good news, you don't have to read all those books or go to all those meetings anymore."

"You," her voice wavered for a moment, "you made such a big decision without talking to me? What if I don't want to do the show in 4 years?"

"I just ensured our future. But I didn't sign your name. If you don't want to do the show anymore, it's fine, whatever. I'll find somebody else to be my co-star. I was just expecting your blessing, maybe a little love and support after I told you I was having surgery. It's exceedingly dangerous."

"Well, I'm not your Mom, you don't need my blessing. You are a grown man who can make his own decisions. Do what you want." Sam got up and left the room; she was on-board.

If you recall my not-at-all made-up account of the surgery, you'll know it was a monumental success. Because Ultimate Frisbee was the main inspiration for my progression along the line of human evolution, it would be fair to expect a grandiose recount of my time with Trey-Trey. We played frisbee together; it was awesome. Unfortunately, fans loved the episode where I chopped my arm off, more than the episode where I played a lawn sport for an hour. I focused on the former; it's what the public wants.

In my wholly accurate and not-at-all dramatized account of the procedure, Sam was conspicuously absent. That's because she wasn't by my side during my life-threatening surgery. Sam decided not to participate for some unknown reason. I mean, she gave me permission and seemed totally cool with everything, but apparently, she was upset about something.

Chapter 8
The Other

As amazing as I am, no story can rest on the shoulders of one mechanical man. The bible didn't just follow Jesus around: it jumped between several character's perspectives and subplots, always with a common thematic through-line. This book is no different. Knowing more about the people in my life will make you appreciate and understand my struggles and triumphs all the better.

Just to clarify, I'm not saying I'm Jesus. That wasn't my point. Although, for the sake of narrative—if somebody in my story had to be the Jesus character—I'm just saying, maybe there are a few parallels.

Sam was the unwavering steady presence I needed. She understood the best way for me to grow was for her to stay completely the same. She understood the concept of a rising tide lifting all boats and/or jet skis. I was the rising tide. I was also the jet ski. Sam could be the boat, I guess. Sam was my compass, showing me the way forward. Unfortunately, I would occasionally neglect to reference my compass and wander through the woods, convinced I knew which way was north. The sun always sets to the left. Here's an example of Sam being a boat, or North Star, or compass, or whatever.

Random Fan: You're that guy from that show.

Me: And you're nobody. Do you even have your own TV show? Leave me alone.

Sam: Hey, that's kind of rude.

Me: Fine. We can take a picture, small child. I'm sure it'll be your life's greatest accomplishment.

Sam was able to keep everything in perspective for me. Be kind to fans because that's where the money comes from. Sam was responsible for making sure we sensibly spent and invested our money. We would go over the credit card statements at the end of the month, and she would say things like, "You can't fund another underground rap album. These just don't have the return on investment you think they do." Or "If you keep buying treasure maps from mysterious travelers, you will end up broke and cursed." But money is meant to be spent, so the best I could do was reduce the number of chances I took with my volatile financial investments. All it takes is one gold record buried on a desert island to make it money well spent.

I had been able to convince Sam to join me in this adventure by promising a better life. And I delivered. Sam would often insist her life was "actually not that bad" before the unexpected windfall. She claimed she could have been happy living a traditional life. This is something ignorant, poor people say. Money makes everything better. I can't imagine her waking up every day, going to work in an office, making small talk with equally insignificant people, and coming home to her cats.

I've explained to Sam numerous times why this is not a real way to live, but again, she persists with this ludicrous notion that being normal is okay. She's not a normal person: she's special. Begrudgingly, I told you how smart Sam is, but the world didn't appreciate her back when she was a "regular." When she graduated from college, she did so with expectations of changing the world. The idealism she possessed was noble, albeit naive. Within six months, she was working for a bank, contemplating arson. But the bank only leased the building, so really there was no point.

Contrast that with her life now. She's rich. And while I am willing to concede money isn't everything, it sure as hell is a lot. Money doesn't make you happy, but money can buy things, and things make you happy. Money doesn't help you be a better person, but money helps you pay the bills, and not having to worry about having your electricity turned off gives you more time to be a better person—theoretically. Here is a list of things Sam was able to accomplish with money from the television show:

- Buy a car.
- Start her own non-profit connecting orphan cats with orphan humans.
- Something about business that I can't remember. She either got a business degree, started a business, or killed someone and stole their business.
- Extend her youthful good looks for a good 10-15 years longer than the average person.
- Not have to be subservient to Brenda, the Branch Manager.
- Buy a second cat. I told Sam she should buy one of those expensive cats that are pretty but also really bitchy. Instead, she got a rescue cat that's pretty but also really bitchy.

And what's the alternative to a life of excellence? Ending up like her parents: content with the simple things in life? Disgusting. We visited them for Thanksgiving, and I discovered some horrible truths. Something so vile, I became worried for Sam's future well-being.

Picture the four of us at a long wooden table. If possible, picture a wooden table made from pretentious wood. Sam and I, on one side, her mother and father on the other. Behind them was a giant clock, the kind of clock that had a pendulum mechanically rocking back and forth. There is a certain kind of person who owns one of these clocks: an old person, more specifically, an old person who thinks they're too good for modern technology. A digital clock would serve the same function without any unnecessary translation.

"Sam, your mother, and I are worried about your long-term plans. What are you working on?" said her father, George.

I had to interrupt, "I don't understand the question. Sam's doing the TV show with me."

"We know, son," said George as if he was a wise judge, and I was just some delinquent in court for vandalism, "but no show lasts forever. We just want to make sure Sam is taken care of when the time comes."

I had never considered the show ending as a realistic possibility. The idea people would stop loving me was upsetting, so I pushed all related thoughts deep down where they couldn't hurt me. Eventually, those issues would surface, and I would have to deal with them, but I don't want to say much more about it at this time. Nobody likes spoilers.

"Well, I've been preparing for that eventuality." Sam saying "eventuality" was a bit jarring. "I've asked Grace, the producer, to let me shadow her. I've learned a lot about the day-to-day logistics required to keep a show running and profitable, as well as the larger strategy to monetize."

Her mom, just like the clock, was very condescending in her response, "Yes, but you're talking about TV. What about the real world?"

"You don't think the principles transfer?" Sam asked. "It's all about market research, product distribution, and marketing. We found out there were many people in New Zealand illegally downloading the show, so we set up distribution rights and produced an episode about New Zealand culture: the one with all those sheep. But I can see you're concerned. You'll be pleased to know I've also been taking classes towards my MBA. I'll be fine." The whole evening made for very dull content. I'm glad Sam didn't let the cameras come with us.

"You mean, *we'll* be fine," I said.

"Yes. Of course," said Sam.

Sam's parents seemed to be satiated with her response. It was then time for them to turn their concern towards me. "And what about you?"

"What about me?" I asked.

"What are you doing to secure your future?" said her father.

"This will ensure I will always be relevant." I waved my arm around—the metal one.

"How so?" asked her father.

I couldn't believe he asked me that question, so I immediately got out of my chair, ripped my sleeves off, and walked over to the patronizing grandfather clock. I lifted the clock over my head in one swift motion. "See what I mean? I don't think we have to worry about the show getting canceled."

"Confusing turn of events aside, everything ends," said her mother. "And even if it didn't, I can't imagine you would want to do something so empty for the rest of your life." It became clear, her mother embodied everything I hated about that stupid bitchy clock.

"I don't understand. Our show matters. You know, you've seen it. Our show is culturally important. Some might say groundbreaking," I said with the freestanding time device still hovering above me. It would have been impossible for Sam's family not to be impressed with how strong I was.

Her father responded with something so shocking and vile I immediately dropped my mortal enemy to the ground, smashing into hundreds of smaller, yet still condescending, clock pieces.

He said, "Well, no. We don't watch television programs. In fact, we don't even own a television set."

My concern should be quite evident by now. These people are weird and unnatural. If Sam thinks she can be happy as someone who reads books instead of watching TV, then maybe she is lost, and I can't help her.

Chapter 9
The Two-Parter

A staple of every great sitcom and reality show is the vacation two-part episode. This is where you go to a remote, beautiful part of the world and vacation like royalty. The vacation episode serves several purposes. First, it allows your viewers at home to go on a vacation; God knows they are probably impoverished and have never left the crappy city in which they were born.

Second, it gives your show a change of scenery; they see you in the same setting over and over again, and your message gets old. But if the viewers could see me drinking alcohol out of a coconut and wrestling with a monkey, then they would remember I am a singularly unique talent. Their adoration for me would be renewed.

Third, the storylines write themselves: "Couple," in the most beautiful place you've ever seen, enjoy a once in a lifetime experience. A mundane problem occurs, which will threaten to ruin their entire trip, such as the loss of sentimental jewelry. "Couple" fights despite being on vacation from their problems. Problems are not like animals; you can't just kennel them before you leave. You have to make room in your carry-on bag. "Couple" deals with their issues before the end of the trip and still get to have one last excursion to a romantic waterfall.

Fourth, and most important: free vacation!

Our two-parter was no different. We arrived in the Amazon ready to begin a whirlwind adventure that would inspire us to be better people. We went through the motions with the show. It started with a tour in what I can only assume was the touristy part of the Brazilian rainforest; I didn't even see an anaconda eat a jaguar. I did get to meet a semi-domesticated Toucan who tried to steal my watch. I assumed he was part of an elaborate jewelry crime ring, but when I questioned him, he played dumb. All this made for exciting TV.

I am trying to remember the "fight" Sam and I had. I believe it involved me "flirting" with our tour guide. I may have been mad at her because she had been giving me poor directions and almost got us eaten by a sloth. Either way, we pretended to be angry with each other before we staged an apology. Here is the entirety of the argument and resolution condensed and summarized.

Me (on airplane): We're on an airplane.

Sam (in Brazil): We are now in Brazil. Look, a toucan.

Maria (with an accent): Hi, I'm your tour guide, Maria.

Sam: You think Maria is cute. You're a pig.

Me: Do we go left or right?

Sam: Left.

Me: Oh, no—a sloth.

Me: I'm sorry for looking at the tour guide. I should only look at you.

Sam: I overreacted.

Me: No. I overreacted.

Both of us: Oh, look—a beautiful waterfall.

Me: Have you seen my watch?

We made up in time to take a canoe ride down some river, possibly the Amazon River, but I can't be sure. We ended up at this waterfall, where we both told each other how much we loved each other. The only problem with all of this was how fake it was.

When we arrived in Brazil, we were obligated to work. But our reward for a job well done was time to ourselves to explore. We made our way along a remote path that had become overgrown. We stumbled upon an ancient civilization that had been living in isolation since the beginning of man. Maybe not the very beginning of man, but like, a long time ago. How old you ask? I don't know—super old. I've provided a sketch to give you some idea.

History of Existence

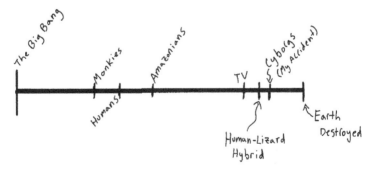

The timeline provided clearly establishes the tribe as an ancient people with many archaic traditions: like growing and eating their own food and worshipping deities. This tribe had been isolated from the rest of the world. We weren't even allowed to bring cameras with us; I was the most advanced piece of technology they had ever seen. They never advanced with the rest of the world, and it wasn't our place to push them forward as a society (according to Star Trek). As to why they never advanced: I assumed it was because they were a dumb society full of intellectually inferior people, but the more I thought about it, the less sense this made.

Maybe it's more likely society advances by accident. You need to have the perfect conditions and the necessity to develop into the monstrosity that is the human race. And maybe this ancient civilization never had proper motivation. Their life was so damn satisfying they never asked, "Is there more?". And when I think about it, it does seem like a perfect existence. All they do is eat tropical fruit and exotic animals in between having sex and sunbathing bottomless by waterfalls. Occasionally, they'd get eaten by a giant snake, but so is life. I wouldn't have evolved into a super mecha-human if I didn't have the whole "getting hit by a car" catalyst.

The human race is so advanced because it was so very dreadful to be a human for so very long. When we started, we were near the bottom of the food chain. It was like our first job was in the mailroom, and we had to develop a killer instinct before we could ascend to CEO of the company. Once we advanced to become the kings of the world, we realized how boring life was when you didn't have to worry about getting eaten by a hungry, hungry hippo. That's when we invented science. Science led to inventing old age. Humans were becoming older and older until they realized something: being old sucks. So, we continue to advance as a species until we create a 200-proof alcoholic beverage that tastes like water, and until we can negate the effects of aging. Dull the boredom and live forever.

Life sucks, and we need to advance until it doesn't.

So, what is the point of all this? Well, when we met the villagers, they got a glimpse of my legs and assumed I was a god. I wasn't supposed to reveal them, but it was hot, so I turned my pants into shorts. They were the Ewoks, and I was C3PO doing magic tricks. Oh man, did the Jedi take advantage of those Ewoks. They manipulated them into thinking their God wanted them to go to war. It was messed up when the English and French did it during the crusades, it was messed up when Middle Eastern extremist did it, and it was messed up when Luke Skywalker and C3PO did it. Little Lisa Ewok didn't have anyone to tuck her in at night because her dad died fighting The Empire.

Did I ruin their society by showing them my true form? Maybe, but at least I didn't get them shot with blaster weapons. Oh well. Once they advance to the video game level of sophisticated society, they'll thank me.

Afterward, Sam and I were being driven back to the hotel. We needed to rest up and shower before getting back to work. We still had to shoot the big fight scene before the day was over. "That was fun, wasn't it?" asked Sam as a sun-scorched man, with a big bushy mustache, dressed from head-to-toe in khaki, sat at the wheel.

"Yeah. It was nice, but of course, the proud people of the Kuntsu tribe ended up worshiping me as everyone eventually does," I said.

Sam scowled. "You're joking, right?"

"If I were joking, you'd know it," I said. "Because you would have paused to decide if what I said was racist and then realize it wasn't. Then you would have laughed. Did you do those things?"

"I love you, but you've been getting a little full of yourself. Maybe a little egocentric. And honestly, I'm getting a little tired of being just another planet orbiting you." Sam stepped on the accelerator of a metaphorical sports car and went from zero to sixty instantaneously.

It was my turn to respond, and with all real battles, I had four options. I could have chosen to attack, defend, use an item, or use magic. I decided to defend. "Why are you trying to fight? We were sitting here, having a good time, talking about our amazing vacation. And then all a sudden, 'look at everything that is wrong with you,' 'you're not a god.' Just stop."

"If I don't point out your flaws, if I don't tell you you're turning into someone else, who will? My job is to make sure you stay the person I fell in love with."

"I am a complex person. Complex people grow, they evolve. I can't just be stagnant like you." I attacked.

"I'm constantly trying to better myself," said Sam. "I'm taking classes. I'm sitting in on production meetings, so I have a skill once the world gets tired of your novelty. All you do is figure out a way to get more attention."

I sat there for a second, hoping to calm my raging emotions. I am often a victim of my own feelings. "You weren't complaining about me getting more attention when it meant you could quit your job and make a living off me." It was another attack. You know, I heard myself saying it and was immediately filled with regret.

"Dude, what are you even saying?" Sam asked.

Time for some magic. "I would like to take my last statement back and say something different." She buried her face in her hands like a jaded wife buries a pillow over her spouse's face while they sleep. I assumed the gesture meant my spell had worked, and my previous statement was erased from her mind. "Millions of people love me just the way I am. I'm an inspiration to those people. They appreciate me. Some even worship me for how I overcome adversity every day. I am a humanitarian. And if you can't see the value in that, I'm sorry."

"Why would anybody worship you? You're just a guy. You don't do anything special. You're just like everyone else," said Sam. People are so dramatic sometimes, which is so annoying I've devised various plans to kill all humans.

I'm a relatively amiable person and generally non-confrontational. I'm like a teenager getting pulled over by the cops for speeding but who is more concerned with the large jar of weed in his trunk. Typically, he only buys it in sandwich bags, but he got such a good deal it would have been fiscally irresponsible to buy anything less. "Yes, sir. I was speeding. Good eye." But like a renowned baker, Sam knew how to get a rise out of me.

"How dare you," I said. "I am nothing like anyone else. I am a fricken hand-woven poncho sewn by blind nuns in Mexico."

The driver with the big bushy mustache turned towards us. "Not to interrupt, but we are pulling up to your hotel now. Although, if you are looking for one-of-a-kind clothing, I know a one-eyed, one-legged, one-armed, no parent orphan who makes some cool shirts. But don't worry, he makes it with armholes on both sides."

Sam put her hand on the door handle for dramatic effect before turning to me. "You're just a man who got hit by a car and now thinks he doesn't have to follow the rules of human decency and compassion. You're not a hero; you're just a narcissist with a TV show." And since her hand was already on the handle, she opened the door and exited in one swift motion.

"Can I give you some advice?" asked the driver. He had put the car in park and had fully turned around in his seat.

"Yeah. Why not?"

"Buy her a gift," he said as a toothy smile crept across his face indicating how proud he was of his advice.

"What?" I asked.

"Are you married? Buy her a ring and get married. For-giveness guaranteed," said the driver. "I've only seen a woman that upset once in my life. It was when my girlfriend found out I sold her car and used the money to travel to the world's greatest water parks. When I returned home, after a whirlwind affair with this water slide operator, she wanted nothing to do with me. Much like you, I was at a loss for what to do."

"I didn't say I was at a loss," I said.

"Here's what I did," he said. "I sold the pearl earrings she kept hidden away in her bedside table. Beautiful, expensive, family heirloom earrings. She had gotten them from her mom, who had gotten them from the grandmother, who inherited them from her grandmother's dad. Why her Great-Grandad had pearl earrings, I couldn't say. I suspect he was a pirate of sorts, sailing the seas in high fashion. Anyway, I sold them and used the money to buy her an engagement ring."

"I don't think my Sam's self-esteem is low enough," I thought out loud.

"It took a lot of diligent work over the years to systematically destroy Rosaline's self-esteem, but you're missing the point. It's about the gesture. It was clear I thought long and hard about how to make her happy. She recognized that." This sociopath was strangely unabashed.

"Since you're obviously a monster, what happens when you do something terrible again?" I asked. "You can't get married again." Call it morbid curiosity, but I couldn't pull myself away from this deranged man's story. I had no intention of heeding his advice, but it's always good to hear different perspectives.

"I've had three kids, and I was unwilling to have a fourth. It's the reason I'm now divorced, but I had to draw a line somewhere. It's important to set limits in a relationship." The driver mimed, drawing a proverbial line in the sand.

"Well, sir, I guess you've given me something to digest. I'm gonna go." I slid to the door.

"Wait. One more thing," said the driver before I could exit his vehicle. I turned back to face him. "The fare was paid for by the studio. Tip not included."

I reluctantly reached into my pocket and pulled out what seemed like a moderate amount of the local currency. Like every brunch ever, the product I received was not worth what I ended up paying for it.

It was interesting, however. The driver's advice was to use items to end a fight.

Chapter 10
The Romance

It is not every day a man gets to realize he has to get married. It's an exciting time in a person's life where they look at the beautiful woman they're currently sharing their life with and decide they want to be with that person forever. And the only way to achieve this goal of eternity is to give up and get married. Sam is that woman.

You might be thinking I am crazy to let an old shuttle driver from a remote part of the rain forest influence my behavior. You'd be right. Fortunately, my sanity is intact. I am of sound mind and choosing to get married of my own volition. I am not trying to make Sam forget our fight or that she was angry at me; selective mind erasing equipment was not readily available. Consequently, let me tell you about the most beautiful proposal you could ever imagine.

It starts with a glorious Italian dinner in Italy, where I order in perfect Italian with a flawless Jersey accent. After, we walk along the Venice canals, where we end up in a helicopter. The helicopter flies us to Paris, where I have reserved the Eiffel Tower for our enjoyment. We go to the top floor where there are two million rose petals on the floor. An average looking woman, covered in flower petals, plays the violin more elegantly than a CD of the most elegant violin playing songs. Why is she average-looking? You don't want your target to feel threatened. Also accompanying the fiddle maestro is Lars Ulrich (the drummer from Metallica.) Once we step onto the top floor, Morgan Freeman comes from around the corner and starts to recite the most beautiful speech you've ever heard. When he finishes, he jumps off the tower, and hopefully, I remembered to pack his parachute. But there is no time to tell if his chute opens on time because I am aggressively on not one, but two knees. I spout poetry. Her breath has been taken away, absolutely gone—gasping for air. After a medical professional performs CPR, I present a beautiful pair of diamond-encrusted slippers. These are the slippers her Great Grandmother was able to hold onto through the Holocaust. I ask her to marry me; she says yes. Lars Ulrich drops an otherworldly drum solo as we make more passionate love than anything you've seen on the internet.

My actual proposal was similar. I couldn't get the producers to shell out the cash required to execute my plan exactly, so I had to make some concessions. Instead of the fancy dinner in Italy, someone made us spaghetti we ate back at our place. Instead of the Eiffel Tower, we went out to the outdoor patio. Instead of the violinist and Lars, I put on a playlist I found called *Love Songs to Put Her in the Mood*. And it turns out her Great Grandmother didn't own any diamond-encrusted slippers and grew up in Detroit, which I heard was nowhere near the Holocaust—a real letdown. The Holocaust slippers pulled the plan together.

"Sam, would you accompany me to the patio?" I needed to usher her into position on the main stage before I could blow her mind; slyness was paramount. I wanted this proposal to be like a 2x4 to the back of the head. Sam thought this was a quiet dinner, just the two of us. She had no idea what was coming;

what an idiot. She also had no idea everything was being filmed. The producers and I decided to keep all the cameras hidden to get a genuine reaction.

"You're starting to get a little weird," said Sam with distrust painted across her face. "And since I was against coming over in the first place, maybe it would be best to call it an evening."

"No, no, no. Just step outside with me, I want to ask you something." Women like to be blindsided with stuff. She followed me to the patio where fireflies were lighting up the sky. Not fireflies, small lightbulbs in a bottle—same difference. I took Sam's hand by my human claw and got down on one non-human knee.

"Samantha Eloise Chrysanthemum, will you marry me?" She stood in silence, which I could only assume was a "silence of joy." The longer the silence lasted, and the longer she stood as still as a burglar who just realized the blind man he was robbing woke up, the less confident I was the feeling overwhelming her was joy. "Did you hear me? Should I repeat it?"

"No. No, please don't." Sam sputtered out of her catatonic state. "Did you really think...do you honestly believe marriage...what are you thinking?"

"Oh, jeez. I thought you'd say 'yes.' And like a fast 'yes,'" I said.

"Seriously? I moved out as soon as we got back from Brazil. We haven't even spoken in two weeks," said Sam. I began to formulate an alternate plan as it became clear she required a bit more convincing. I thought it would be best if I rose to my feet.

"Yeah, just because you needed space," I said. "You've had space. We should celebrate by permanently removing all space."

She looked at me like I was a moderately tricky mathematic problem: impossible to comprehend. "I don't know what to say."

"I mean, you said leave you alone. But that you just needed time and then we could get back together. I've given you time," I said.

"What I said was," Sam's trademark gesture had been to bury her face in her hands, "'leave me alone and don't call me. I need to decide if I want you to be a part of my life.' Second, you called me five times a day. And that's an average. One day you called fifteen times."

"Well, yes. Fifteen is a bit excessive, but I can explain most of those. The first five times I called were to tell you how much I missed you and how I wanted to be with you. The next five were admittedly unnecessary. I had gotten angry because I could have been calling about something life or death, like your grandma dying, or my grandma coming back to life, or an epidemic of unexplained grandma deaths and resurrections across the country. But you wouldn't answer. So, I kept calling to see if you would answer. The next three were because I felt bad, and I wanted to apologize. The next call was because I couldn't find my phone and you were always good at helping me find it. Finally, the last call was to tell you I found my phone—it was in my hand the whole time. Does that help?"

"I've loved you for a long time, and you were my best friend. I can't marry you." Sam paused. There was no malice in her words, and all the aggression disappeared from her face. The only appropriate way to describe Sam's expression was sadness. "I don't think we should see each other anymore."

There is no way I can express to you the emotions I felt when she said this, but since I'm writing a book, maybe I should try. It hurt, like a whole lot.

"Slow down there, Seabiscuit. I don't know how we went from marriage to breaking-up. Put a pin in it. Let's all take a deep breath to get all the crazies out of our body." I shimmied. Sam did not follow my lead. "Have you talked to your mom? She'd tell you to marry me."

"My mom advised me not to come here today, and I should break-up with you," said Sam.

"Your mom's a dirty bitch. Don't listen to her," I said, trying to elicit a reaction from Sam that never came—uh-oh.

"I don't think there is one person I could talk to who would think marrying you was a healthy and smart decision," she said.

"Isn't that what makes it exciting?" I asked. "If I was getting married and nobody thought it was a huge mistake, if nobody was trying to stop me, what would be the point?"

"Well then, how we ended up here makes sense." I realized I had been clasping her hands, holding them close to my chest, close to my heart—*beep, boop, beep*. I became aware because Sam began untangling herself. She took a step toward me and planted a sweet, slow kiss on my forehead. She whispered as softly as possible, "I gotta go. I hope you find the type of admiration and love you crave, and I hope it makes you happy."

She turned and began to leave. If she wasn't aware before, she became aware of the cameramen that filled the house. She quickly weaved her way through the crowd and out the door. They had descended on the living room so they could get the perfect shot. I'm sure they got it.

I couldn't tell if Sam was crying because the tears in my eyes made it impossible to see. It was like looking through the windshield of an old car with broken wipers on a rainy day. I was crying and alone—well, not alone. I became hyper-aware of the half-dozen people that were being paid to document and broadcast my pain to the world. It's possible they were also crying, but I couldn't be sure through my defective human eyes. Here's a small consolation. This episode got excellent ratings—the highest for any single episode of our show.

Chapter 11
The Opposite of Romance

Let's get this out of the way right off the bat: I was not sad. Our amicable decoupling was the best thing to ever happen to me. I am a desirable guy, and that's what's referred to as a fact. If some people can't understand, then the hell with them. Like the $50 in bar money awarded to a wet t-shirt contest winner, I am a prize worth fighting for. It was a blessing for several reasons. Most importantly, it allowed me to start the competition up again. And like no time ever before in my life, there was a line out the door of beautiful women waiting to be doused with icy cold water.

Unlike the previous woman I was in a long-term relationship with, many of these ladies valued the fame and exclusivity I brought to the table. I don't want this to be one of those things where I exploit the female gender for my personal gain. Anyway, here are the famous women I was "connected" with in the tabloids: Veronica Jetten, Natasha Korvinco, Haley Smith, Judy Wallin, and Hannah Barbacoa. You read correctly: one actress, one singer, one professional softball player, a girl I used to have a crush on in middle school, and a famous model. Okay, the girl from my childhood was not famous, but it's something I would like everybody to know. Thank you, former roommate, with whom I used to share a bed. You freed me and made all this possible.

Free time seems to increase exponentially once you become single. I put all my newfound energy into the friendships I neglected when I was in a committed relationship. We've all been there. There just aren't as many occasions to fly spontaneously to Vegas on a Tuesday night when you have someone waiting for you. The big winners of this break-up were my boys. Congratulations, boys! I put together a little entourage to rival the fellas of *Entourage*, all centered around a robotic Vinnie Chase and Germ as my right-hand man.

It's imperative to get a good group of people you can trust. If you can't trust them, that's okay too, as long as they bring something to the table. I feel like I nailed the formula with my group. Have a guy to generate stupid ideas, have a guy who has all the hook-ups, and have an intimidating guy that can operate as a fall-man, if necessary. And most importantly, they all understood I was the biggest star, and I was in charge.

This was just for the main crew—the guys you invite to the Hollywood parties. There were a few others I kept on the payroll to serve necessary functions in my life. These guys didn't get to go on many fun adventures. For example, I had a person who helped me dress hipper, a person who handled day-to-day transportation, and a person who was really good at geography. I'm not sure who hired these people. One day they would just show up, and I would give them a job.

> Me: *Who are you? What do you do?*
>
> Rotten Milk Joe: *I'm Joe and whatever you need.*
>
> Me: *Can you drink some of this milk and tell me if it's rotten?*

Rotten Milk Joe: Yes! From now on, I'm your rotten milk guy. That will be my sole purpose—to stop you from drinking sour milk.

I didn't have to pay Germ, Nailgun, or Skippy Peterson. They were my friends and we had cultivated the perfect group dynamics. Let me tell you a story that should serve as a guideline for all emerging celebrities in need of an entourage. We came up with a plan to drive from Mexico to Alaska. We were in Tijuana partying and thought to ourselves, "You know where I've always wanted to hang out? In an Igloo."

Me: The thing about Mexico they don't tell you…

Nailgun: It's hot.

Me: Exactly

Germ: We should go somewhere. Where is it the opposite of hot?

Nailgun: The cold.

Germ: Yeah, you get what I'm saying.

Me: We should totally go to the cold guys.

Skippy Peterson: When I was 18, my show had just gone off the air. I decided to go into the wild. So, I took some acid and rode the train up to Alaska. I ended up burying my people's Choice Award in an igloo beneath the ice-coffee table of an Inuit woman.

Me: Dude. I'm super into igloos.

Skippy Peterson: Wouldn't mind getting that People's Choice Award back.

Our plan was set. We would make an incredible journey to expand our minds and commune with nature. Igloos are natural occurrences in nature, right?

Let me give you a rundown of the crew. Germ was my boy, but he also brought a lot to the table. He was our hype guy and our idea-man. It was his idea to embark on the trip, but it was also his idea to buy our drugs in Mexico before we crossed the border. The drugs were cheaper in Mexico—probably an import/export tariff situation. You take the good with the bad, I suppose.

Skippy Peterson was a former child star from one of those network sitcoms. We were able to watch him grow up before our eyes. Unfortunately for him, going through puberty in front of millions of people was not an enriching experience. Skippy is always trying to get back into the limelight, which is exhausting. Skippy knows just about everybody in Hollywood. He may not be popular, but man do people want to give free drugs to their favorite child star. I knew Skippy the same way everyone else knew Skippy: through TV. I didn't meet him in person until we both appeared on a celebrity game show. Or rather it was a pilot for a game show. They couldn't get enough people interested because it mainly consisted of pseudo-celebrities trying to invent new types of uses for everyday household items. I was never clear why, but everyone had to wear skin-tight bodysuits. Either way, Skippy took his paycheck, and we went clubbing. Overall, an enjoyable experience.

Nailgun belonged to Skippy. He was, as his name suggests, tough as glass. I think they met each other in juvie or at like a miniature golf course detention center. From there, Nailgun graduated into real crimes. I'm not sure what he did, but he went to prison for a month and came out with a reputation and a shaved head. And unlike his head, where hair would eventually grow and alleviate the baldness, he couldn't seem to shake the reputation. He became Skippy's closest confidant and protector. When he was around, people would think twice about making fun of Skippy for being a loser, which he was. That's the crew: a moderately attractive group of males with a penchant for women, partying, and being famous.

After the four of us were detained by the border official as we attempted to reenter the states with freshly purchased drugs, and after being released by a very happy and very bribed border official, we made our way north. Being giant celebrities, we, of course, became distracted by the offerings of the common people. We made a stop about 100 miles up the coast in the beach city of Newport Beach. Here, a couple of the most gorgeous women an average person would ever see in their lives (they were only 7 1/2's on the celebrity scale) told us about a yacht party happening on Will Ferrell's legendary Sex Yacht. It was rumored his whole deck was lined with tiger fur, and all the doors were fashioned from panda bear hides: the two most sexy animals in nature. We figure the people of Igloo Town, Alaska could wait.

Like good party guests, we arrived inebriated, taking the burden off the host. The legend himself did not personally attend these events; he did, however, teleconference in. His face was on every television on the boat, where he video chatted as a proxy for partying himself. Word on the street, Will Ferrell was prohibited from partying by his wife, children, and agent due to the damaging, albeit probably hilarious, adventures he would get himself into. I can't imagine what a pre-neutered Ferrell party was like considering how awesome his remote parties were.

He was surprisingly still very involved in the festivities despite lacking a physical presence; he made comments and gave directions from his TV throne. There were monitors and cameras in every room on the boat, even the bathroom and the hook-up room. Will Ferrell was a pervert. When you're at the bar, and you hear him yell "turn on the lights, I can't see anything," it's safe to assume he's monitoring one of those rooms— killing the mood. For many people, it was the best night of their lives, and almost everyone came away with a story to tell.

Since I was such a massive star, I thought I would let the women come to me. Naturally, I spent most of the night in a room with a bunch of guys playing video games. We incorporated drinking into the games because we're adults. We were playing a racing game; modifications were made to turn it into a drinking and driving competition—a terrible idea in real life, but a very, very good idea otherwise.

"Pick your character." An older man with hair whiter than Utah sat across from me. We both sat in gaming pods that were Godzilla-sized, egg-shaped orbs hollowed out to allow for entry. His long hair, which matched the pearly white gaming hubs, was held back with a golden headband. He wore a long flowy white shirt with golden snakes stitched into the fabric. There was a lightness to him as words floated from his mouth. It's what I imagine Aristotle or Jesus would look like if they shopped at exclusively high-end Texas thrift shops.

"Shut up, old man, give me time," I said through a burp gurgling up my throat.

"Don't mean to rush you, young man. Choosing who you are in life is the most important thing you can do. Why should video games be any different?"

With Texas Jesus's permission, I took my time choosing the coolest looking digital gaming car. I picked the blue car because it was blue. Also, I was drunk and having trouble remembering the previous options once I had scrolled past them.

Some time had passed before I realized everyone was staring at me, "What? What happened?" There were frustrated faces around me except for Germ; he was laughing.

An intimidatingly gorgeous man with a voice as smooth as silk—no, stupid comparison. What else is smooth? Yogurt? Yes, he had a voice as smooth as yogurt (pre-granola). He sat in the third of four pods that occupied the room. He seemed pissed.

The beautiful man said, "We finished minutes ago, and we've just been waiting for you, but you're too drunk, and you're just going in circles. I don't like waiting. I imagine this is what women feel like when they are waiting for me to commit, but I won't do it. I am just too beautiful to let one selfish woman monopolize me. The point is, it's unpleasant. You need to either finish the race in the next 10 seconds or get yourself up out of the gaming pod."

The stunning, half-Jewish, black man was right; I should have probably called it quits. I should stop playing video games and start romancing the ladies. I'm sure I could find some young tech-savvy groupie, but instead, I threw up in my pod. I stepped out of the egg-shaped orb through the back panel after leaving my shoes in the puddle of vomit. Why would I want them anymore? They were mostly for show; the alloy coating of my robot heel was impenetrable.

I could hear noise from all around. I couldn't make out who exactly was yelling, but deductive reasoning would indicate it was everyone. What I can tell you is the yelling got louder after I wandered over to the other side of the room to apologize to the golden seer and the very famous recording artist who had just chastised me. I promptly projectile vomited across the room—a messy affair.

I don't know if it was because I had thrown up on nearly everybody, including a Grammy award-winning musical artist and possibly Texas Jesus, but I came to the realization I was drunk. People were not sympathetic and were seriously uncool about it. You know who had absolutely no chill was Will Ferrell. Come on, dude. Just buy a new boat. Preferably one with a dry cleaner on board so Lenny Kravitz doesn't have to walk around the party smelling like vomit.

The least drunk member of my posse, Nailgun, saw security start to mobilize and began shepherding us off the boat. To this day, I am unclear who did it. On the way out, somebody got their hands on a harpoon gun and shot through a vase into a priceless work of art.

"Get em' out of here!" Will Ferrell could be heard yelling from his digital throne. "How dare you! Don't you know who I am?"

Don't feel bad; these were rich people, and they could afford new art. We expeditiously invited some girls to leave with us before the cops showed up—no luck. We walked off the docked boat and into the night looking for beautiful young women or at least some Taco Bell.

We found neither. We did stumble across some horses, but for legal purposes, I will not say where we found them. There were four; I got a horse, Skippy got a horse, and we made Nailgun and Germ share because it was funny. Oh boy, was it funny.

I don't generally like living things like animals. I usually feel much more comfortable with cars or Segways. But riding drunk into the night on Asimov's Delight, I felt at peace. As the vibration put me to sleep and emptied my bladder, a sense of calm overcame me. We rode through the darkness away from everything and everyone. Like a cowboy in the wild west with a flashlight, I hoped to ride my steed through the night and into morning. Eventually, we came to a road, which led us to an overpass where we dismounted. I'm not sure what happened to those horses. Maybe they found a wild and free pack of horse brethren with whom they could start a new life. Or perhaps they found their way home—they are nature's autonomous vehicle. I'd like to imagine Asimov's Delight, Elon's Obsession, and Mr. Kloppy Klopp accidentally rode into the street, got hit by cars prompting emergency surgery—resulting in a new species of super horse cyborgs. A highly comforting thought.

"How you feeling, man?" Germ asked. He seemed not to be listening to my internal monologue.

"Peaceful," I said peacefully.

"Do you want to spit over the edge on to some cars?" He asked.

"No, no, I'm fine," I responded with a butt-load of Zen.

"Do you want to throw up over the edge onto some cars?" Nailgun asked.

"I would love to." So, we took one more shot of whiskey or tequila or whatever, and I leaned over the edge. My eyes started to water, but I could hear my insides make contact with modern civilization's version of a horse. I once again felt connected to society. Anyway, this is the story of how Nailgun spent some time in jail for stealing horses and throwing up over a highway—allegedly.

Chapter 12
The Ethical Dilemma

I know what you are thinking, because I have heard it before, "you are the death of the human race." And I'd be lying if I told you I never laid awake at night, contemplating what it meant to be the bridge between humanity and machinery. If you think about it long enough, there is only one logical conclusion: my wiring and CPU will eventually convince me the most efficient way to interact with humankind is to exterminate them. And again, I would be lying if I said I never thought about how I would kill all humans.

I settled on digging a bunch of giant holes. I would fill them with different addictive items like free iPhones, People Magazine, Mountain Dew, french fries, cigarettes, and hard drives filled with porn. When people came to investigate, I would dump a bunch of dirt over the vices. I realize how dark a reveal this is, but the electricity would occasionally seep into my brain filling my head with many impure thoughts. Mere mortals needn't worry; I didn't have the manpower to coordinate wide-spread hole digging and dirt dumping—I abandoned it.

I had never been part of a minority before. And now, I wouldn't exactly say I am part of a minority; instead, I am the start of one. Either way, I am different enough to receive vitriol and hate from the majority. And to be clear, the majority is the human race—historically known to be jerks. Just look at the dolphin. Actually, you can't because the humans started to get jealous and systematically exterminated the dolphin. They were getting a little too smart and a little too organized. When it became clear they were talking about us behind our backs—end of the line. They're gone.

I empathized with the dolphin's plight. I got a little too advanced a little too fast; people felt threatened. I know I shouldn't read through all the internet threads about myself, but it's hard to resist. All the mean things people would call me: "an uglier C3PO," "a more annoying C3PO," "not actually a robot if you look up the definition of robot"—it got me thinking. Am I a different species: Robosapien? Or am I an evolved part of the human race? Will I spark people to follow me, to better themselves by integrating their cells with circuits? An experience that helped me understand my place in this world and my responsibility in creating a better tomorrow.

I had a lousy month awhile back. My drinking had steadily increased to an all-time high. A few tabloid hit-pieces described my behavior as "increasingly volatile." They couldn't get enough of one incident, in particular.

I was at this club, and a guy started to get real aggressive towards my group. I have never been one to back down, so I told him what I thought about him in not so pleasant terms. I was probably a little harsher than I needed to be. I had all this pent-up anger and frustration, and I just needed to release it. I unloaded on the poor guy. As was his right, he punched me. Unfortunately, he punched me somewhere I had recently upgraded. He hit what was equivalent to a steel wall and shattered his hand. Don't worry—I felt terrible. I immediately went out and bought him an expensive fur coat to make amends. Also, don't worry;

it wasn't real fur. It was some fake faux fur I found at some progressive store. Soon after, the store from where I bought it got caught in a sting operation using child labor to make their clothes. That one is on me, my bad.

Not the biggest deal in the grand scheme of things, but the week after, the paparazzi caught me coming out of a strip club. In an inebriated state, they caught saying something unflattering about a specific religious group. Don't worry—not the one you're thinking of. My agent and manager were afraid I was getting a bad reputation, so I visited a school to counteract the damage I had done. I was supposed to speak to them about what it means to be a good role model and how important it was to stay clean.

I walked into the classroom, and they all just stared at me the way only kids do, with unabashed boredom and indifference. I was used to stares, but I wasn't even showing off my arms or legs. They would have had no way of knowing I had more in common with their washing machines than their parents. Kids have always made me uncomfortable. I think it's because I have a lead-paint based personality (not suitable for children.) Or maybe because when I looked at them, I realized I was growing older and am oh so close to death; twelve is the new thirty-one.

"Hey, kids. What's up?" I greeted the classroom full of what I can only assume was sticky children. They stared back at me with blank faces, so I turned to the teacher. "What is this, some sort of career day?"

"Sure, if you want it to be," said their teacher, who was just as indifferent as the children. "Any lessons you can teach the kids. You can just talk about what it is you do and how you had to work hard to get it. Or maybe some trial or tribulation you've overcome."

"I got hit by a car. Should I talk about getting hit by a car?" The faces on the students lit up in excitement, probably because of violent video games.

"Yeah. Whatever," said the teacher.

I looked around the room, trying to find comfort in something. The children sat with intrusive silence, not allowing me to gather my thoughts.

"Who here has heard of TV?" About 75% of the hands went into the air. "A bunch of cord-cutters. I can respect that. Well, I am on TV, and I am extremely famous."

A little girl in the first row raised her hand. "Are you an actor?"

"No. I'm just on TV. And I am famous because I am on TV," I said.

"Do you have, like, any special skills that qualify you to be on TV?" asked the girl.

"Well, I am just an interesting person, and people want to see me live my life. No, wait. There is something special about me." I ripped off my pants to show off my hardware—I often wore tear-away pants to make dramatic reveals. The "oohs" and "awes" exploded from the crowd. We were getting somewhere.

"Yeah, I have mechanical arms and legs," I said.

Oh, I forgot to mention: I got my other arm replaced for symmetry purposes. I was now a zero armed, zero legged incredible robo-man. No one was around to tell me it was a bad idea, so I just kind of went for it. I considered getting an additional four arms because I loved Spiderman, but I decided against it—one arm at a time.

"Pretty cool," a young boy offered his praise.

"It is pretty cool, yeah. There's more, though. I use these arms and legs to do super cool things. Do you guys know

Demarcus Lewis, the chess player? Well, I once beat him in an arm-wrestling match with my robot arm."

The little girl in the front raised her small hand again. It is unfair to single out her hand as being small—her whole body was exceptionally tiny. I pointed at her bestowing the gift of speech. "How did you become like that? Was it through hard work? My mom says if I work hard, I can be anything I want to be."

"And what do you want to be?" I asked.

"A veterinarian. I want to take care of animals," she answered.

"Well, I didn't exactly work hard to become like this. I was hit by a car." They loved the bit about getting hit by a car. What an audience.

"So, you are famous because you are on TV and you are on TV because you were run over by a car," said a little boy (who probably had distinct features with which I could describe him, but I won't.)

"Technically, only my legs were run over," I said.

"You got famous by accident then?" Said a different little boy in the front of the class. This one was chubby.

"Yeah, it was easy," I said.

The smart little girl in the front raised her hand once more. "You didn't have to work hard, and you made a lot of money. Sounds like a lot more fun than being a veterinarian! I want to be a robot too!"

The whole class started screaming, "Me too! Me too! Team Robot!"

If there is one takeaway from this story, it should be my power of persuasion. I convinced an entire class to become robots in just under five minutes. I would not be one of a kind. I started the world down a path to which there was no return—

kind of like a steep, slippery slide covered in oil. I know what you're thinking: you can climb back up this slide. No, you can't because I also set the slide on fire.

When you are staring at the extinction of your own species, by your own hands, it makes you stop and think: if I were sending a terminator back from the future, where would I send them? I put some serious thought into this. If I sent them to kill me before I became a slightly smarter version of the Roomba, then they would just put these legs on the body of some other less charismatic version of me. It may take this dreary wannabe longer to convince people to turn their backs on their sisters, brothers, wives, children, dentists, etc., but they'd get there eventually—the tech is undeniable. I would have died for nothing.

I considered other moments in time in which to *Terminator* the robot apocalypse. I could have them kill me soon after I've made the change—a promising, yet flawed proposal. If I were murdered, it would only expedite my sainthood, transforming me into a martyr. It would be just like that one guy who tried starting a new religion. He was killed, and it only validated his crusade. You know the theology I'm referring to—the one based on the Lizard King and alternate dimensions.

Me dying was not the answer. There was another way; there was someone else who would need to die. Possibly the man who invented electricity or the man who invented robots: George Lucas, I think. Maybe we could kill that little girl after she made the transformation. The uproar of a tiny human girl dying could put a stop to this whole process. Maybe it would be enough if I sent my messenger of death to kill my doctor. He wouldn't be able to invent me, and he wouldn't be such a drag on human existence—problem solved.

As you can see, this is something I took very seriously. I had a few contingency plans if I ever needed to save humanity; This includes the extermination of all of Florida. They've been holding back the human race for too long. And most importantly, none of these plans would result in my death, which is the whole point. The longer I could go without dying, the better.

This isn't some pointless thought experiment. It helped me arrive at a world defining conclusion: if humans can't keep up, then they will be left behind and eaten by the pursuing tigers known as progress and time. And if they figure out a way to stop the inevitable evolution of existence, then they deserve the earth. I dreamed a dream of humans and machines coexisting on equal footing, but as the inferior species, it's up to them to take the necessary steps.

Chapter 13
The Rival

"Everything is all set," said Grace, my stern and fragrant producer. "He just wants to talk to you first."

"Does he speak English?" I asked.

"That's not something you're allowed to ask; it's offensive."

"Offensive to whom?" Offending people is inevitable, and rarely do I burden myself with the easily outraged, but it's always nice to know who you are offending. That way, you won't be surprised when you receive hate mail.

"To people who do or do not speak English. Just don't ask." Grace filled the role of protector since my previous partner had abandoned me. I felt like she always had my back, or at least had her investment's back.

"How will I know if he understands me?" I asked.

"He'll respond."

I have so many stories and so many episodes I could talk about. I could tell you about my failed foray into the world of country music. Actually, no. Thanks to a non-disclosure agreement I signed, I can't tell you about my time in Nashville. I could tell you about Hurricane Felipe killing all those people. A fantastic tale of death and heroism, but I'm barely involved. A fruitful natural disaster for me personally, but perhaps not the best story—we can do better.

Those stories are too positive. Up until now, my life had been a rocket ship of success. But what happens when a rocket ship gets too close to the sun? It falls back down to earth. That's why I need to tell you about Hinata 3000. Stupid name, right? He sounds like a futuristic LaserJet printer. Hinata 3000 was actually the most popular human cyborg Japan had to offer. We thought we could use him to fix everything, but unfortunately, that plan blew up in my face—much like a rocket ship when it gets too close to the sun. Public humiliation is the next logical step in my journey.

I was jumping from party to party, from model to model, from anecdotal story to anecdotal story. But these forays into the seedy world of yacht parties (and the world of avoiding certain celebrities because you threw up on their carpet at a yacht party) masked a fundamental truth: I was becoming less and less relevant. The high point of my popularity came during the proposal episode, but ever since, our ratings had been in steady decline. I didn't get it. The show was essentially the same before and after (aside from replacing a very unlikable character.) We tried everything to rekindle the audience's interest: I got a dog, I got married and divorced (same weekend), I got a haircut. We did everything we could think of, but people were bored with my antics.

My team came up with a solution to put me back on the cover of US magazine (a hurtful gossip outlet.) But this time the headline would read *Super Awesome Robot Celebrity Isn't an Embarrassment to Humans and Household Appliances Everywhere, We Were Wrong.* Or something like that. We decided we needed to extend my influence to a global audience. We considered several markets. Germany would love the cold efficiency of my artificial body parts, but we didn't think they enjoyed humor or drama—they were out. We considered England, but I always had trouble understanding the accent—they were out. Luckily, there was a place that respected their celebrities, a place that respected technology. That place was Japan, and Korea, and any other country that might be in Asia.

The idea was simple, a classic crossover episode with my Japanese counterpart. I would grow an audience overseas and finally be worshipped as I deserved.

"Hey, dude. How's it going?" I said through a magic device that transmitted my words and sounds across the globe. "I heard you wanted to talk so we could discuss a collaboration."

"Oh, is this a collaboration? I thought you were trending toward obsolete, and you needed me to save you? Or was the situation explained to me incorrectly?" Well, Hinata 3000 spoke English.

He was mean, but he wasn't wrong. And I couldn't respond harshly in kind because the truth was, I needed him. But if I let him walk all over me, he would have all the power in our relationship, which would be a problem. He who has the power has the power—so the saying goes. I had to walk a thin line between reverence and disdain.

"The way I see it, this is mutually beneficial," I said. "You are going to get as much out of this as me."

"How do you figure?" he asked.

"Where would Apple be without Microsoft? Magic Johnson without Larry Bird? Taylor Swift without Katy Perry? Red without the color blue? Everyone needs someone to push them to be better. Everyone needs a rival." I know I should have only listed three examples, but I had too many to limit it to just three—day versus the night. I had hoped I could get his competitive juices flowing.

"The Japanese without the Chinese. Americans without obesity," Hinata said, adding to my list.

"Sure. You get it. We'll push each other to be better, and the audience will respond."

Whether it was for dramatic effect or if he was contemplating how he wanted to proceed, Hinata paused before he said, "I already have a thriving following. I don't need you."

"How naïve. Let me explain something to you. You're famous now, but tomorrow you could be replaced by a younger, hotter robot or even a cartoonish world leader refusing to let others share the spotlight." Sorry, I couldn't think of a third example. "You need to do everything you can to protect yourself before you're just another entry on Wikipedia. Do you guys have Wikipedia over there? It might be called something different. It's like an encyclopedia, but on the internet. Do you guys have encyclopedias? It's like the show Jeopardy, but in book form and sorted alphabetically."

He paused again to consider my warning. I'm speculating and editorializing a bit. He could have been making a sandwich. I had no way of knowing. "Japan and America may have been on opposite sides of the Lizard King's Great and Bloody Crusade, but I think it's time for our countries to come together. And I think we can start the healing process," said Hinata.

"Truer words have never been spoken. Okay. I'll see you on the other side of the pond. May the Holy Lizard grant you safe travels."

"And a sun-soaked rock to warm yourself to you," he said.

The crossover would happen, and I had no reason to believe it wouldn't go according to plan. We would have some light-hearted banter followed by heavy-hearted banter. He would teach me about the true essence and spirit of a robot and how to make Robot Sushi. I would show him the joy American excess can bring and, of course, the true meaning of Christmas.

Hinata 3000 greeted me at the airport. The first part of the series would be him immersing me in Japanese culture, and the second part would happen back in the USA—there was never a second part. It was clear from the moment the cameras started rolling; he had no intention of sharing his spotlight. Instead, he wanted to steal my market share like I was the soul of a Native American, and he was a camera.

> *Hinata 3000: Look who it is. Mr. America.*
>
> *Me: Yup. Happy to be here. Get me out. I want to see the people; I want to see Japan.*
>
> *Hinata 3000: Yeah, I bet. Probably never even left your country. Probably don't know where you are.*
>
> *Me: We're in Japan. Right?*
>
> *Hinata 3000: *says something in Japanese**
>
> *My Translator: He says, "Stupid American whipped cream canister."*
>
> *Me: Dude. What does that mean?*
>
> *Hinata 3000: Come on. I'm going to take you to show you what a real robot is and how you will never be one.*
>
> *Me: Uh. Okay.*

Everything he said was designed to subjugate me to him and paint me as this American idiot. Let me address something controversial. Yes, I am an American; I love fried foods and exclusively speaking English; I don't know if the Middle East is in Europe or Asia, and I love throwing recyclables away in the regular trash. But I am not a fat American. Wait, did he call me fat? I mean, I'm not stupid.

More importantly, he wanted it to seem like I was less of a robot than he was. I understand there are people out there who are smarter than me—I could live with being called an idiot. But the idea that he was more of a robot than me—laughable. Not only were all my appendages of the metallic persuasion, but also, no one had championed the rights of robotic humans as I had. I was the one who sued a local coffee shop; I was the one who yelled at the boy scouts; I was the one who set that flag on fire. All furthering robo-mecho-human rights. Hinata showed a complete lack of respect when he kept referring to me as a canister of whip cream (metallic on the outside and white boy on the inside.)

There wasn't too much footage I could use. We had to heavily edit around his constant barrage of insults.

> *Hinata 3000: That's called Sumo Wrestling, and your tech is ugly and poorly integrated.*

> . . .

> *Hinata 3000: That's called Nintendo Factory, and you're stupid and not funny.*

> . . .

> *Hinata 3000: That's called Mount Fuji, and your parents never loved you. They told me.*

It wasn't all bad. It did get me a few extra fans and introduced me as a more sympathetic character. The words cold, mean, and kind of a dick kept coming up in all those focus groups. But compared to Hinata, I was compassionate. In a vacuum, sure, not a terrible plan and execution. But if you looked at the aftermath and what it led me to do, hindsight and all that, I wish it never happened. Maybe Hinata was more of a robot than I was, I thought. Maybe, I wasn't good enough. His incessant negativity had me believing I was unworthy of the mantle I had put myself on. Who was I? A machine or a regular ol' dumb human?

The only worthwhile human contribution man has given this world is machines. I could never live if I thought I was part of the perpetual monotony they call human life. Like someone confronting their image in the mirror, jiggling their neck flaps, I knew I needed to go under the knife. Replacing my arms and legs weren't enough to satisfy the world. I needed to do more.

I had options. I could choose to replace my ears to give myself super-hearing—to better hear what people think about me and to hear people's conversations on airplanes. I could replace my nose so I could more intently smell my garbage and public restrooms, or I could replace my voice so I would sound like a computer. I did the first two things plus a few bells and whistles. I got a touchscreen integrated into my arm so I could monitor my vitals and watch kick-ass snowboarding videos whenever I wanted. I also got an actual whistle to protect myself if I ever got confronted in a dark alley. Talk about regrets; I looked like a Picasso painting. These surgeries were a push off a chairlift, which gave me uncontrollable speed down a mountain. And once I reached the bottom of the mountain, there was no guarantee the chairlift would be able to take me back to the top.

Hinata is just a footnote in my story. I will be remembered, and he has already been forgotten. This journey towards remembrance and immortality came at a price. A price worth paying? Only time will tell—no, it wasn't worth paying.

Chapter 14
The Abyss

Everything is cyclical. Maybe not everything, but certainly fashion, trends, and time, and also perhaps love. There is no denying I had just gone through an unprecedented era of love and esteem. But unfortunately, the admiration someone like me receives from the general public ebbs and flows. Bears understand the lukewarm behavior of man; it's why they hibernate every winter. Man's love of bears ebbs during the winter and bears act accordingly. I have grown to realize it was unrealistic for me to expect to be the center of attention forever. But hand to God, I thought I would live for all eternity, harvesting everlasting energy from the adulation and eyeballs watching me. That little run-in I had in the previous chapter was because I wasn't ready to accept any ebb whatsoever. Call it poetic justice, call it irony, or call it something that more accurately describes my situation, but my resistance to change made things worse—like vaccines and seatbelts.

What happened to me was a tale as old as time: like a love child between a KitchenAid and the Titanic, I kept adding more gadgets and functions until I eventually sank into the ocean. I did not look good with my new additions, and, honestly, for the first time since my metamorphosis, I found myself uncomfortable in my skin. Part of my discomfort was because I didn't look like me anymore. When I looked in the mirror, I no longer saw an enormous nose that had been a magnet for ridicule in my younger years and a hindrance to side-facing pictures in my later years. I no longer saw my Dumbo ears that made front-facing pictures also a difficulty. They were aspects of my face which I had no love for and readily dispatched. My new nose and ears were to be a couple of no-nonsense tools capable of performing their designated function. They came without any of the baggage of natural-born features. During this effort of self-improvement, I realized something: my nose pulled my whole face together. It drew the attention away from everything else wrong with me.

The other reason I no longer felt comfortable in my own skin was because it no longer was my own skin. I mean technically, I did own it (they even gave me a receipt); I just didn't make it myself. Normally, the body is self-sufficient, producing the necessary energy to function with the help of fruits, vegetables, and cupcakes. However, there was not enough energy to power all the beeping and buzzing. Apparently, electricity needs to come from somewhere, and my body could no longer sustain the excessive load I produced. They presented me with a couple of options to fix my hardware problem. One solution involved batteries and charging myself every morning. I operated this way for a while, but inevitably I would forget to plug myself in at night and wake up without the ability to hear or smell. Plus, I kept losing my charger, and it was exorbitantly expensive to get a replacement because it was made exclusively by Apple. This was an unsustainable daily routine.

Option #2 was an expensive pair of overalls. No one cares if their overalls get stained with paint or damaged, and they are ugly as all hell—that's the point. The basic concept was I would replace most of my skin with this new synthetic material. Your skin is a magnificent organ, but the drawbacks are numerous. It burns, it's susceptible to cancer, it gets dry and itchy, pimples erupt from it like some sort of erupting mountain, and of course, it is used as a weapon to discriminate. These were some of the rationalizations I told myself as reassurance that replacing my sunburnt prone skin with energy-absorbing, ultra-protective skin was the correct decision. Think of my skin like a solar-powered calculator. It would absorb energy while I was sleeping, and when it was time for the day to begin, I would have a full reservoir of power to allow me to hear the rooster crow.

I said the trinkets on my face were not very visually pleasing aspects of my appearance—understatement. My new skin couldn't have looked worse even if it had been replaced with a quilt-like compilation of old skin recovered from a local burn ward recycling bin—also an understatement. I have never been someone who lacked self-confidence, but it was only because I was perfect, and it was justified; I suck now. Blind confidence in one's self is the most valuable trait a person can have, aside from an above ground swimming pool filled to the brim with liquid money. But sometimes the neighbor you hate because he has everything in the world you wish you had, is incredibly unhappy. And I'll tell you; all my neighbors hated me for a myriad of reasons.

I don't want to scare you guys, but things got insanely dark. And when I say "dark," I mean Stephen King telling his wife of 50 years he doesn't love her anymore after she becomes blinded during a Solar Eclipse. I didn't leave the house for weeks, they tried to continue with the show, but it was impossible to get enough footage and a decent story when their only setting was me in a bathtub filled with cold water and warm urine. Eventually, the crew disappeared for what they called a "temporary hiatus." The word "hiatus" reminded me of the word haiku, so I wrote many a haiku to express what I was feeling.

> Frankenstein's Monster
> Except he is a robot
> Good movie idea?

I don't know if the two are related, but me writing and performing my feeling poems coincided with my friends disappearing.

Skippy Peterson and I were friends, but it was a shallow companionship. We were together to maximize fun and to increase our proximity to fame. We rarely had a sober conversation about our innermost hope, dreams, or fears. Now that I think about it, we may never have had a sober conversation just in general. When Skippy left, so did Nailgun. Like divorced parents splitting up their children, I got the one I liked best, and Skippy got the one he liked best.

"I know you're going through a lot right now, but I can't handle all this negativity," Germ came to me one day with some sob story. He hung around just long enough to appease his conscience before abandoning me. "It's bringing me down, and I'm actually in a good place in my life. I'm seeing someone nice, and she's helping me take care of my life. I'm not stealing anymore or committing any felonies, just the occasional misdemeanor. I don't want you to think I'm abandoning you because you're not successful anymore. That's not the case. We think you're a bad influence on me, and Marissa thinks we need some time apart. But I want you to feel free to call me if it's something super serious. You're still my best friend, think of it as us going on hiatus." I was left alone with only my money to keep me company.

No one loves me now
Didn't I once own a cat?
#WHERSMYCAT?

My piles of money gave me runway to do absolutely nothing. Weeks stretched into months, and months stretched into different months. Isolation is dangerous because when your main companion is yourself, you start to realize how much you suck. I learned a lot about myself during this period of hibernation: I am the worst human being in the world and have zero worth to anybody. The days bled together. I don't even remember how I filled the time. I know I must have eaten; I probably watched TV; bathroom visits must have taken up three-four hours a day. I don't remember doing any of those things. I do recall sleeping constantly with utter disregard for when the sun was in the sky—not that I would have noticed. I made sure the curtains in my room blacked out any semblance of light. I would crawl out of bed just long enough to drink some water and possibly pee before I returned to bed.

I wasn't always sleeping, but I felt comforted, wrapped up in all those blankets like a burrito. Maybe it was an evolutionary feeling reminding me of a simpler time being swaddled by my mother. Covers protect you from the outside world; it's a proven fact. I remember as a kid, I would sleep with a blanket draped over my head to ward off serial killers. And you know what, we can argue correlation versus causation all day, but I never got murdered. The bed spread I used now was a much more expensive and softer blanket than the one that protected me as a child—it came with a higher protection rating. I would try to keep the crying to a minimum, but I could no longer control my emotions, the harder I fought, the deeper I sank into my self-inflicted dark bedroom.

I tried to go outside one time, to venture back into the world, but it didn't go well. I saw a squirrel I thought might want to be my friend. But he, being a squirrel, rejected my friendship. It was unrealistic to expect any other outcome, but I was extremely fragile at the time. It's hard to explain, but this squirrel represented every rejection and every negative life experience I ever had. The squirrel was the coach who cut me from the team, the parents who were disappointed I didn't become a lawyer, the girlfriend who thought I was too immature, the other girlfriend who thought I was too immature, the boss who fired me for stealing socks, the girlfriend who said I had an appropriate level of maturity but was too boring, and the squirrel was Sam.

I often found myself thinking about how I got to such a low place. The road was a winding one, but I kept following the road signs as they led me spiraling down into hell. I thought about if this current situation could have been avoided. A lot of things had been out of my control. A man isn't responsible for the person they become; my environment shaped me into the man I was—simple behavioral psychology. Nor was I responsible for the life-altering trauma turning me into the world's greatest infomercial for robot appendages. I'll concede I made mistakes and the occasional selfish decision. Could I have acted more empathetically? Sure. If I thought about Sam's needs and desires before I thought about my own, would she have stayed? It's dangerous to get into hypotheticals. Perhaps if I were a different person, I would have gotten hit by a truck earlier on the timeline before the technology used to save me existed—classic butterfly effect situation (the butterfly effect says you shouldn't go back in time because you might get eaten by butterflies). That's why I try to avoid hypotheticals.

I needed a way out of the dank, plunging well of self-loathing, and didn't have a rope, ladder, or jetpack to facilitate my escape. Every so often, when the sun was directly overhead, the light would shine on me—giving me a brief period of respite. I would use this time to plot my future and plot my escape, but soon the sun would pass, and I would be left huddled under the covers.

What I required was help. But the people I had relied on my whole life were nowhere to be found. I needed Germ, I needed Sam, I needed my manager, I needed my style coordinator, I needed my hip-hop slang teacher, I needed my rotten milk consultant, but I would be damned if I called any of them. If they were real friends, they would have instinctively heard my silent calls for help. They would have come without me having to ask. They were fake opportunists and no friends of mine; they were seriously played-out and wack. But then again, I wouldn't mind seeing Rotten Milk Joe one more time.

I am the Tin Man
All the world is the Scarecrow
I miss my Dorothy

Chapter 15
The Mentor

One morning I heard a knock at the door. Usually, I let these things go to voicemail, but I was scouring my kitchen at the time, trying like hell to find some waffles. I walked over and looked through the peephole hoping it was a delivery person I had preemptively called to bring me waffles. Unfortunately, the younger me from the night before didn't have the forethought to order ahead—another day older, another day wiser. Through the peephole, I noticed a shimmering golden man waiting patiently. I opened the door.

"Do you need me to sign for something?" I asked with the expectation of breakfast.

He examined himself as if trying to understand my question, "No, I don't need anything from you."

"Who are you?" I asked.

"I'm a friend. We've met before, but didn't exchange names," he said. I tried to rack my brain for where I crossed paths with this glowing orb of sparkling energy. I was confused—I didn't have any friends left.

"I'm not in the mood for a guessing game," I said. "Could you just tell me who you are and whether or not you have waffles? Then we can move on with our day in disappointment."

"I'm sorry, do you have a busy day ahead of you—somewhere to be?" He looked me up and down and added a condescending glance into my home. My face did not react to his jab, mostly because my facial expression effectiveness was down 75% since the reconstructive surgeries. He continued, "Okay, well, we met at a party awhile back. We played video games together, you were rude to me, and then you threw-up on me. Don't worry; I didn't take it personally. The subtext of your actions were loneliness and suffering.

"Wait, are you Lenny Kravitz?" I asked.

"No," he said.

"Okay. You must have been the other one: Golden Jesus." He was there when I put Will Ferrell on my death list. He was every bit as Golden Texas Jesus as I first described and more. Maybe not more, because Golden Jesus is already a bit of an exaggeration.

"I appreciate the endearment, but my name is Larry," Golden Jesus had his hair tied back with a bandana and wore gold-embroidered track pants.

"Your parents named you Golden Jesus-Larry? Weird."

"I am here because a friend of yours wanted me to come and help you," he said while standing on my welcome mat. Maybe this obligatory sign of hospitality is why he spoke with such bluntness. "You've become an artificial person, and I promised I would help you become the man you are supposed to be. You're Diet Coke, and I want to turn you back into uncut Colombian cocaine."

This reveal should have made me happy—I guess I did have a friend out there—but instead, it filled me with anxiety. Were people out there thinking I was so broken I needed someone to take care of me? Did people gather in groups and talk about what a disaster I had become? I stopped myself from asking who the friend had been. Like Schrödinger's cat, if I didn't ask who sent him, it could have been anyone. It could have been Sam or Germ who sent GJL. However, if I asked, and it turned out to be Grace trying to preserve a business relationship, I would be devastated. Better to keep the mystery.

"Well, come in then. You're just in time. I was about to take a nap for the next couple of days." I said, finishing the work of the mat and welcoming GJL into my house. For a while, he just examined my living space. I should have felt a violation of privacy, but now would have been an arbitrary time to put up barriers. If he was judging me, he didn't let it show on his face. "I know what you're thinking. But you're wrong. I'm doing just fine."

"You seem to be projecting some feelings. I want you to know I don't see any difference between us. We are both just people. Yes, yes, you're a person," said GJL. "A radish is just an apple grown under peculiar circumstances. If the radish had the advantages afforded to the apple, it would be just as celebrated and baked into pies as the apple. Your environment matters. Eat this apple." GJL handed me a radish.

I played along and took a bite. "It's bitter and hard."

"Sounds like your perception of the apple is the problem, and you need to stop judging this fruit based on what you think it should be. And let it exist."

"Everyone in the world knows radishes taste like literal garbage," I said.

"Don't let others perception of you cloud your perception of yourself," he said. What a confusing segue.

"I'm not sure what this has to do with radishes, but this whole thing has begun to bore me. Also, not completely clear why you're here."

"It's a bit of an over-simplification, but think of me as a life coach—Larry: Life Coach to the Stars," he said. "I'm here to pepper you with metaphors and life-lessons until you've been rehabilitated."

"Metaphors? I don't know what you heard, but I'm fine. So, sorry, but I don't need your help," I said as I attempted to usher him towards the door. He slipped out of my grasp and ventured further into the house. He threw open curtains flooding the living room with light. GJL stood in silence and stared out the floor-to-ceiling glass windows.

"What are you looking at?" I asked.

"See that garden you have in the backyard?" He asked.

"Can't exactly call it a garden," I responded. "It's just a fake banana tree surrounded by a bunch of dry dirt and dead plants."

"You shouldn't think about what it is, but what it could be," GJL said as he refused to break eye contact with the backyard. "You see, you are the dead plants covered in dirt. I am the banana tree. The tree is there to encourage the rest of the plants to grow. To be an example of how to live their lives. You just need to follow my lead."

"I feel like I'm repeating myself a little bit. I don't need you," I said.

"Is that why you are by yourself? Or are you by yourself because you've pushed everyone who has cared about you away?" GJL asked.

"Everyone who left me is probably worse off than they were before. Germ is undoubtedly bored. My producers are probably pulling their hair out without me, and Sam's probably reading a book somewhere, poor and dead—freeloading parasites.

"All your friends are doing just fine. Let's see." He pulled a small notebook out the satchel draped across his body and flipped to a page for reference. "Your friend Germ is doing terrific without you. He has a beautiful wife, and has used his fame to jump-start his career as a real estate agent in Manhattan Beach, CA."

I wondered how long I had been here. Didn't Germ just leave like a week ago? Or had I been isolated for much longer? It's hard to tell the passage of time when you break all the clocks in your house and throw away your word of the day calendars.

"Sam is thriving," said GJL. "She started a new career producing new reality shows. Some of the popular shows she has gotten off the ground include *Are You My Mommy?* and the even more popular *You're Not My Mommy.*"

"Yes, but is she dead?" I asked.

"Who else had you mentioned, your producers? Well," GJL flipped another page of his tiny notebook, "Grace Stein has half a dozen shows on the air, that have nothing to do with you. She also is an executive producer on all of Sam's shows. It turns out, they've formed an extremely fruitful partnership. How about doctor—"

"Don't say his name," I said.

"Well, the man is a doctor with a thriving practice and biomedical company. I would be shocked if he even remembered your name."

"What's your point?" I asked.

"All you do is blame other people for your problems. But the truth is, you're selfish." GJL walked over to the fridge and grabbed a beer off the door. "Can I have one of these?" He proceeded to remove the bottle cap using the decorative spurs on his boots—kind of badass.

"Awesome. Everyone is happy, and I suck," I said. "You're bad at this whole life coach gig. Is your goal to strip me of all the self-worth I have left? No, I'm sorry to interrupt. You're doing your thing. Go on, tell me what else is wrong with me."

"Okay. You're entirely too focused on assigning blame," said GJL.

"Sure," I said, "but that's not my fault. I got hit by a truck several years ago."

"What happened to you is not important," he said. "The key to self-improvement is not focusing on yourself, which brings me to the solution: tutor some kids, build a hospital in Mexico, feed the homeless. Your spirit wants to grow like vines on a wall. But when we are too self-centered and self-obsessed, we stymie the growth. By focusing on others, we remove all roadblocks, and our spirit is free to spread its wings."

I decided to perform a little thought experiment. Let's say I rejected his premise: I'm selfish with low self-esteem and a tendency to blame others for my problems. Let's say I take away his beer and kick him out of my house. Where does that leave me? I would be right back where I was: sleeping 18 hours a day and prank calling people pretending to be their dead grandmother. Maybe I would pull myself out of this self-destructive cycle due to sheer boredom. Or perhaps, like James Cameron exploring the decaying remains of the Titanic, I would sink to depths man was not meant to go.

That leaves me with the other option: build some stupid poor orphans a house. Let's say GJL was right, and this manufactured selflessness would lead to real growth; everyone would immediately see how wrong they were about me. Germ and Sam would come back, obviously. Everyone would be like, "We were so wrong about you," "We promise to watch your show; here have some money," and "Yes, I will totally marry you; will you put a baby in me." Minimal downside. Worst-case scenario: I just built a vacation house in Mexico.

You may think I would be too proud to ask for help. You'd be wrong. I'm famous; I expect people to go out of their way to help me—it's their duty as ordinary people. No famous person can get through a single day without the help and support of normies like you. You all are the real heroes.

"What about my hideously grotesque face? I don't want to be seen like this," I said.

"Recall the parable of the radish and the apple," said GJL, "and what it says about self-confidence."

"You're right. An apple does not concern himself with the opinions of radishes," I said.

"Close enough."

GJL was a man of his word. He helped me turn my life around through hard work and expert time management. GJL was there when I woke up (he forced me to wake up), he was there when I washed the parts of my body that were still able to smell (he forced me to wash the parts of my body that were still able to smell), and he was there when I transcended my natural state of egotism and arrogance (he forced me to transcend my natural state of egotism and arrogance). He dragged me back out into the public to do good unto the world. We started out small: GJL took me to a filthy soup kitchen filled with hungry people. This was a low stakes foray back into society. Feeding the homeless is the ultimate act of altruism because they don't have televisions.

> Me: Hello, poor person, would you like me to give you food?
>
> Poor Person: Um, sure. Thanks.
>
> Me: Now, I don't want you to be confused. I know that this is a soup kitchen, but I'm about to serve you chili. It's not a mistake. Sometimes soup kitchens serve other things.

Poor Person: Okay.

Me: And thank you for not saying anything about how famous I am or asking for a picture. That's not what this is about.

Poor Person: Okay.

I was just like Robocop, defending the world with my technological advances in the hopes of getting my family back. (Was that the plot of Robocop?) It was all very therapeutic. With each adventure, I regained a little bit of confidence. Building homes for orphans in Mexico is the ultimate act of altruism because my network didn't broadcast in Mexico.

Me (to a group of orphans): Thanks to us, you now have a place to sleep, and I was happy to do it with my only reward being peace and enlightenment.

Orphans: *something in Spanish*

Me: Hey, do these kids really not have parents? Like any of them?

The Adult Orphan in Charge: Yes. They are all orphans.

Me: Well, I want all of you to think of me as your father. Not in a legally binding sense but more in "I'm a father to all that come after me" sense.

Orphans: *something in Spanish*

Spending countless days with regular people of the world, I no longer cared whether or not my face and skin made me stand out. I had lived amongst them, and realized something important: who cares what they think? They aren't special or interesting, like me. I'm special.

"I'm ready, man," I said to GJL one day after a productive trip rescuing animals displaced by wildfires. As we did after every successful rehabilitation activity, a town car drove us to the ice cream shop as a reward for our hard work. "Put me on your resume in the success section."

I fully embraced GJL and his attempts to build me back up. The construction process started at a subterranean level. My previous identity was built on a foundation of cottage cheese: my unhealthy relationships with Sam, the adoring public, and my very own legs. But thanks to GJL's regimen of waking up, showering, and helping other people, I had a much more solid base. I was building on the idea of helping others, on a being an extraordinary person platform.

"You've made some progress, yes. You've regained your self-confidence and we've trained you to consider the needs of others. But you've only done so with the help of an external stimulus and promise of existential reward. We still have a long way to go before this new way of life becomes second nature. Don't worry, though. We'll get you to self-actualization—eventually." GJL's attempt to temper my progress was inconsistent with the narrative I had been telling myself.

"What are you saying? I'm basically a perfect person," I said. "I've solved the selfish problem, I no longer live like a hermit, and I've got my self-confidence back."

"The path to self-improvement is a never-ending staircase in a building extending through the sky," said guru GJL.

"Fine. I'm not perfect. Maybe I still have room to improve, but I'm okay stopping at floor 47 rather than climb any more stairs—it's where the food court is. Also, I'm not excluding the possibility of continuing the climb. I'm just saying I'm ready to get back out there and start the next phase of my journey. Also, I wish I would have said floor 69—it would have been funnier."

"You're not ready. Let's just get a scoop of pistachio ice cream and discuss it," said GJL.

"I see what's going on here. You just want to hang around because I'm paying you. I am paying you, right? I never considered it. How much do I pay you?" A famed Hollywood life coach would likely demand an outrageous fee. Was Larry just another leech?

GJL said, "You pay me a fair wage, but my suggestion to prolong our union is because it is what I think is best for you. I could make three times what you pay me to be a part of Shia LaBoeuf's self-help slash creative posse. But I like to finish what I start."

Trust, I thought. I must remember the lesson on trust where we zipped lined through a forest. "I don't want to seem ungrateful because I do see you as a friend, but I think it's time to move on."

"Then, I guess this is so long." He made the driver pull the car over. GJL embraced me, which made me think about the last time someone hugged me, and I truly felt loved. I thought about the cop embracing me on the sidewalk, but that was more of a detainment than a hug.

"Not goodbye forever," I said. "I mean, can't I still hire you on a case-by-case basis: like a party clown or like a scary murder clown charging per hour or per victim?"

"Maybe," GJL said as he exited the vehicle, "I charge a pretty high hourly rate—not really economical."

And with that, Golden Jesus Larry disappeared out of my life: possibly forever. Well, not forever, I saw him a couple of weeks later at a Shia LaBeouf art installation. Shia was letting people throw knives at him as he lay naked, strapped to a spinning wheel. But then I only saw him like five to ten more times from that point on. I was on my own: sink or swim, fight or flight, french fries or onion rings, Tina Fey or Amy Poehler, evolve or let myself become extinct. It was up to me. (see answers at the bottom of the page)

Answers: Swim, Fight, French Fries, Tina Fey, Evolution

Chapter 16
The Reconciliation

I'm not the first person to completely turn their life around. Like all the rehabilitated that had come before me, I had the misguided notion my growth somehow undid the bad I had done. Your actions are permanent, and you can't change the past. I thought because I was now a considerate, well-adjusted man, I could get my old life back. Once an ice sculpture melts, you can't reform it. This begs the question: what was I trying to undo? I regretted a lot in my life. One time I got drunk, fell down some stairs, and broke my collar bone. I regretted all those kids laughing at me in the 6th grade when I didn't know what a handjob was. And subsequently, I regretted getting caught by my parents researching handjobs. All those embarrassments haunted me until my final days. I'm not stupid. I know those are unchangeable events in history—what's done is done. All you can do is learn from the past. As an adult, if someone were to ask me a question, to which I didn't know the answer to, I would just yell, "Of course I know what a handjob is. I invented them," and then I would run away—not going to make the same mistake twice.

Some things (that don't entail time travel) are fixable. I knew, given the opportunity, I would be able to undo Sam leaving me.

I painted the picture of a man who flourished with the freedom to do whatever he wanted. But I may have understated how much I missed her. I'm ready to admit I was nothing without Sam. We were a team. I was a beautiful mound of clay, and Sam was Vincent Van Gogh molding me into something exquisite. Van Gogh sculpted things, right? I was a pile of dry Play-Doh without her. Sure, many women have put their hands all over me since Sam, but none of them were able to improve my shape. I was ready to let Sam mold me into whatever she wanted.

I reached out to her. How was I able to track her down after all these years? I just texted her. She still had the same phone number. I knew it was the same because I called her from a blocked number at least once a day to listen to her outgoing voicemail message.

> *Your call has been forwarded to the voice mail service of [Sam]. You can press 1 to leave a message or wait for the tone. If you wish to leave a callback number press 2. *Beep**

I am an excellent texter. I threw out some classics like, "Hey, was just thinking about you. How you doing?"; "I'm doing amazing. Absolutely perfect"; "We should totally get a coffee and catch up." I've always said the best first dates happen at coffee shops. You don't order messy, expensive meals, and you don't have to waste money over-tipping a waitress (makes you seem like a good guy.) I never tested it, but I assumed cafes were also the best place to win back ex-lovers. I didn't see why the same principles wouldn't apply. I had to lie to Sam and tell her this was a platonic meet-up; if she knew it was all an elaborate ploy to trick her into marrying me, well, she might not have gone. I was confident she would forgive me after I revealed my ruse on our death beds.

My plan was thus: I would invite Sam to a semi-private location, but not too secluded so as not to frighten her. A place that we could get coffee without the dangers of strangers interrupting us—good private. Space, where no one can hear you scream—bad kind of private. A perfect location would help me demonstrate the ways in which I had grown. To that end, I would also be reading a book when she arrived. She would be taken aback by my intellect and say something like, "What are you reading? Oh, a book. How impressive." This tactic will put her off-balance, giving me the upper hand.

"What is this place?" Sam asked as she arrived at my carefully chosen location.

"Oh, this place? It's just a little spot I go to get coffee. Let me get you one." I got the attention of a child walking by. "Little boy, the lady would like a latte, and can you grab us a couple of muffins?" The boy nodded and then walked into the kitchen.

"The sign outside says orphanage. Why are we meeting at an orphanage?" She asked.

"Did you see the rest of the sign?" I asked. "They've named the place after me. That's what happens when you help build a building—time and money. So, I come here to mentor the kids, grab some coffee, and just relax out of the public eye. Sometimes I read. Did you notice I had a book in my hand?"

"Yeah, I did." If Sam was taken aback by my appearance, she didn't let it show. She sat down opposite me, nothing between us but a poorly made clay pot with a single flower sticking out of it. A parentless child made that clay pot, not sure if the flower was grown by a parentless child.

"Just a book I picked up; it's called the *Diary of Anne Frank*. Have you heard of it?"

"Yeah, it's a classic," she said.

"Well, I just started, so no spoilers." The book had served its purpose, so I closed it and moved it off to the side. "It's incredible to see you. Tell me what you have been up to.

I already knew what she had been up to, but I had Sam explain her new job to me anyway. I had her tell me a bunch of stuff as if I hadn't been stalking her social media accounts regularly. But I needed her to share those experiences with me herself. I had been absent from her life for quite a while, and I needed to create a sense I had been there this whole time. Now when she thinks about breaking her leg on that patch of ice, she'll think about me driving her to the hospital instead of that sexy fireman she started dating shortly after.

"Thank you, young man," said Sam to the little orphan boy who brought her a latte—with absolutely no foam art—and a muffin. "What's your name?"

"This little boy's name is Steven," I said before he could answer. "It doesn't matter if you have parents or not, Steven. Nor does it matter whether you are a very famous mechanical man or just a small child. You can be whatever you want to be. We're all the same, you and me. We're all just humans."

"These are scones not muffins," I said in disappointment after the little boy had walked away.

"And tell me about you. What have you been up to?" Sam asked. I had patiently listened to Sam talk about herself, and finally, it was my turn to show her how I had evolved.

"I've been busy," I said. "I dedicated myself to change and personal growth. I realized I didn't want to be the person I was anymore—obsessed with fame with zero regard for the people around me."

She nodded with possibly too much understanding. "Yeah, I heard something about charity work."

"My mentor and I thought if I focused on other people's needs, it would make me into a more empathetic and less selfish person." I recited from memory the mantra GJL had me say every morning, "Other people are just as important as me."

"Did it work?" She asked.

"I think so. And now, I'm ready to get back out there," I said.

"That's amazing. It sounds like you finally have a healthy relationship with fame and wealth. Proud of you," said Sam.

"If I'm honest, I went to a dark place when you left. It took me a long time to rebuild my life. But don't blame yourself. No hard feelings," I said.

"Oh, thank you, I guess. I mean, I don't. But yeah, thanks."

"I just wish I were the caring, forgiving, nurturing person I am now back when we were still together. Who knows, we would probably be married with a little robo-baby. 'Beep-boop, I'm a baby.'" My impersonation of a child who had many mechanical disfigurements made Sam giggle. This was the first time during our date she showed any joy. I had her on the ropes.

"Who can say what would have happened?" She asked. "I think everything probably worked out for the best. It seems we're both doing well. No regrets, right?"

"You seem like you're doing well," I said. "I know I am. In fact, I think it's time I start the show back up. Maybe it's not so much a show about me, but a show about me helping people, or a show about new technologies, or a travel and cooking show. I don't know, but I think it's time."

"I'd watch any of those."

"Well, perfect," I said, "because the show was never really the same after you left. You were invaluable to the decision-making process; you kept us grounded."

"I did my best. I was trying to build us something sustainable," said Sam.

"Sustainable, yes—solar panels, paper straws, when a lawyer says objection. We're on the same page." I inched my chair a bit closer to Sam's so that if she were overcome with emotion, she would be able to reach me. "Which is why I was hoping you would consider joining us—get the whole team back together."

"My life in front of the camera is over," she said without hesitation.

"Well then, just join as a producer. We could use your restraint and your ideas," I said.

"Again, appreciate the offer, but I don't think that's a good idea. But seriously, good luck." Sam finished the last bit of her coffee and sat on the edge of her seat.

"I think I understand. It's not the show you don't want to be with; it's me." I started to feel like this whole attempt to trick Sam into reconciliation was misguided and pointless. She saw the orphan boy, she saw the book, and I told her how well I was doing. What else could she want?

"Why would I want to work with my ex?" asked Sam.

"Next, you're going to tell me you don't want to get back together after all." I moved the chair back to the other side of the table.

"I was hoping you just needed some closure. I had practiced this whole speech about cherishing our time together and always loving you. I would tell you about all the ways I had changed and grown as a person, but I don't think you care about any of that."

I'm not sure why people assume all change is growth. Perhaps the change Sam was referring to made her a worse person.

"Well, I bet I grew more than you did," I said.

"Wonderful." Sam, having no interest in arguing about who grew more, rose from her seat, and prepared to leave.

"Obviously, the whole point of personal growth is learning to be happy with yourself and not relying on others for contentment and all that garbage," I said as I stood from my chair and followed her through the house. Little orphan children were running around, unaware of how bleak life can be. "But neither one of us will be happy without each other."

"I'm happy," she said.

"Jeez, 'happy, happy, happy,' that's all you ever say now," I said.

"Maybe deep down, I wanted to see you too: for my own closure. Maybe that was selfish of me." Sam mumbled as she walked out the front door.

"Sam," I shouted, causing her to look over her shoulder, "see ya around."

"Yeah. Good luck."

I would love to end this story right now with Sam rushing back into the house and confessing her never-ending love for me. The two of us would move to Iceland or somewhere warmer like Cancun. We would share a cottage and live out our days anonymously spearfishing or spear hunting caribou, depending on which of those two countries we settled in. I have the perfect ending: what if someone accidentally dropped a piano on Sam, transforming her into a female robot (is there a word for "female robot")? The two of us would grow metaphorically old together, enslaving the human race by corrupting the world's technology, one sentient vacuum at a time. Sorry to disappoint everyone, but she didn't come back.

Closure may not have been what I was looking for—I was looking to reconnect with Sam—but closure is what I got. I can't blame my plan; there is no way she wasn't impressed with my book. Nothing I did would have convinced her to love me again, which was a comforting thought. I had no choice but to move on. Move on to what—I didn't know. Perhaps there was a girl out there who was in a horrific train accident who was salvaged with technology, someone who complemented me as a person. Maybe my future was a career. I could find a job that allowed me to be loved without the pressure to be a god.

This was the last time I talked to Sam. On her drive home, a piano fell from the sky, killing her. If you end up trying to verify my version of events, you may discover Sam ended up getting married about a year after this story took place. Ignore all that—it didn't happen. Death is better for closure.

Chapter 17
The Resurrection Part II

I know what you're thinking. You're thinking this is where I spiral out of control again. You're thinking I am so fragile I won't be able to handle the shock of my ex-girlfriend rejecting me and then accidentally wandering into an airfield where a wayward antique hydrogen blimp crashed into her like the Hindenburg—I think this is how she died. But this is a success story. I am a fighter, and I am mentally strong. This is a story about perseverance, and it is meant to inspire. No longer was I going to let things I had no control over keep me down. That's what I did when Sam left me the first time, and that's what I did in third grade when Jenny Schlotzky pantsed me. I bring up those events so you can understand what kinds of experiences used to send me into shame spirals. Those are definitely the best two examples I could think of.

This is a story about perseverance and achievement, and for this story to be complete and make sense, I need to ~~kill all humans~~ get back to the top of the public's metaphorical respect mountain. I fell into a crevasse and was forgotten and left for dead. But I climbed out, prepared to scale some icy mountainscapes. Navigating the frozen tundra of relevance sounded easy enough. I just needed to look back to my heroes, who had accomplished the same feat and regained their influence: Robert Downey Jr., Tom Cruise, and Mike Tyson. Whether it was because of drugs, cult affiliation, or eating children or something, these people reshaped their image. Since I had no need for rehab, I would have to emulate Tom Cruise and Mike Tyson.

Like them, I needed to find a hit comedy movie to cameo in. As you are likely already aware, I was the breakout star of the teen sex romp comedy *Too Many Penises in the Pie*. I know what you're thinking, "not another teen sex romp comedy" movie. You'd be right if you were wary of the over-tapped genre. The cinemas were flooded with countless attempts to exploit the raging hormones of the male adolescent. Typical Hollywood: they figure out a successful formula, and they beat the idea into the ground. It's just like how around ten years ago, when every other movie seemed like it was about the Lizard wars. There were a couple of movies from the human's perspective, one from the Lizard's perspective, and another version entirely from the moth men's perspective. There were a few comedies, a musical, and even a dance movie. Each one of these movies seemed to be less original than the last, except for the dance movie, which taught us one couple's passion for dance can stop the killing, if only for a moment.

We may not have been the first to break ground on the Teen Sex Romp genre, but we upped the ante by the sheer amount of male genitalia we showed. Also, ours was the only one to star both Tippy Von der Stute and myself. Tippy was the hottest young star, and I was once again a household name, like the White House. Okay, maybe I didn't star in it, but I stole the show as the uptight camp counselor who didn't know he was working at a camp for overtly sexual gay males. They never explicitly mentioned my non-organic limbs—which was nice—but they did have me wearing tank-tops and jean cut-offs exclusively. It goes without saying, but hilarity ensued. It's why our movie won the Oscar—category: Best Teen Sex Comedy.

Step one, completed. This put me back into the public eye, and this time, they saw me in a more positive light. People no longer watched a TV show centered around me doing terrible things and being self-centered. This movie wasn't about me, and I was okay with being a supporting player. Shortly after that, the opportunities started rolling in. My agent and I decided to accept everything offered; occasionally, our can-do attitude resulted in hits, like with my miniseries on the cooking channel: *Find Out What Robots Think of Your Cooking*. And sometimes the gigs were less than ideal, like when I presented at the Kid's Choice Awards—they dropped this weird green slime all over me. Either way, my name became a staple in the global lexicon just by the sheer volume of work I was putting out into the world.

I was back to dominating the Earth, and this time it would never end. I had an encounter at an airport bar, which left me proud of all I had accomplished. It was Christmas eve, and I had to be in New Zealand the next night for a Christmas show they were putting on. They wanted me to light the tree. A man approached, taking the empty seat next to me at the bar.

"Are you who I think you are?" The man asked, even though it was completely clear I was me. All he had to do was look at my arms, legs, face, skin, or personalized jacket to know for sure.

"Yeah, it's me," I responded. "Are you a fan?"

His eyes widened as he nodded with a bit too much fervor. If we weren't in an airport, where they confiscate all weapons, I might have been worried he was a crazed fan trying to murder me.

"Huge fan. I've watched your show since the beginning."

"You're not the guy who ran me over, are you?" I asked in jest, but also that would be a crazy story twist.

"I wish." he replied. "I learned so much from you. Like, I learned about adversity, technology, and partying, but also how the human race is a dying species, and how it needs to be eradicated." It's a bit surreal when you find out you've genuinely impacted another person, and they understood the lessons you were trying to teach them.

"Thank you for saying all that. It means a lot to me." I finished my drink and was looking for the bartender to order another.

"Sir, it would be a great honor if you would let me buy you a drink," said the man.

"I appreciate the offer, but I kind of want to be alone right now." Would it have been nice to take that man's $12? Definitely. But there would have been the expectation of talking with him further. I valued my fans now in a way I hadn't before. I had realized fans were the only way I could feel alive and loved. This is why I no longer showed outward disdain for them, but that didn't mean I wanted to spend too much time with one. He seemed disappointed. "You know what? How about we take a picture?"

"That would be just about the best thing to ever happened to me. My wife is going to be so impressed, maybe she'll start answering my calls again." We took the picture, and he went on his way with the knowledge his life was all downhill from there.

Later that same evening, another person approached me, but this guy knew me from *Too Many Penises…* and offered to buy me a drink. I let this admirer of mine give me the $12 necessary to afford a beer at an airport bar. I spoke with him briefly about the inspiration for my new catchphrase, "Boys, put down the oil," and then sent him on his way. I then offered the customary picture; he declined but had me record a hologram for his answering machine system.

Now, the question is, what was the difference between these two fans? Why did I let the second guy give me money I didn't need, having just declined the previous man's offer? The answer is simple, the first gentleman was already a lifelong fan. I could have spit on him—I didn't do that anymore—and he still would have been a follower. The second gentleman was a new fan, which is always more important. I knew I was back on my way to the top because this is the first time someone recognized me entirely from my new career; he was unaware that I ever even had a reality show. It's kind of like if someone only knew Arnold Schwarzenegger from politics. My ability to continually generate new fans made me proud and gave me hope for the future.

As I stated, returning to prominence was only the start of my journey. I needed to build a warm place to live on top of the mountain. I had a plan for this as well.

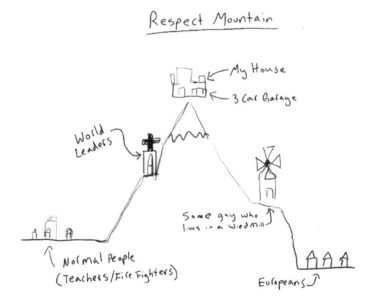

128

I needed some annual occurrence to remind people I was still alive and was still relevant. My inspiration for this came from people like Dick Clark, who kept telling us he was alive every New Year until he wasn't. Also, Jesus, who made us sit in church every Easter and Christmas when all we wanted to do, was get drunk on Easter style Eggnog. If you think about it, Eggnog makes more sense during Easter. Similarly, every year on my birthday, I would take another step in achieving what man has always dreamed of: ~~flying~~, conquering our fragile bodies. I know I made a big deal about looking like a freak, but that was just insecurity in my fading fame and lack of identity.

I was still trying to be human, and as a result, I was this freaky human/robot hybrid. I needed to go further. I needed a permanent, recognizable identity: robot. My inspiration came from another hero of mine: Ariel from *The Little Mermaid*. Ariel was all twisted up. She didn't know whether she was a fish or a human. In the end, she made a choice to get her groove on as a human which gave her happiness. Sure, it took a lot of adjusting going from a fish to a woman. I mean, fish don't menstruate, do they? In the end, she did what she had to do. What I had to do was slowly detach myself from all that made me human. Are mermaids fish or mammals?

Most of my exterior appearance had been replaced over the years, as you know. Have I told you about the time I got hit by a car and lost my legs? But there were still a few outer modifications left to make, not to mention I could always improve the existing technology. I even put my ego aside and called Dr. Gruber.

"So, what do you say?" I asked the doctor after explaining my plan to him.

"Yeah, sure, whatever," he answered.

"Don't you want to think about the ethical ramifications of destroying my humanity? This could be dangerous. Don't you want to weigh the pros and cons?

"No, I'm all set," he said without hesitation. "I got some trinkets lying around here. Do you still have feet? I can give you an electric can opener for feet if you want."

"Why are you helping me? Don't you hate me?" I asked as I paced around my now well-lit house—happy people don't live exclusively in the dark.

"You consider what I'm about to do, help? Oh, my," I imagine he said this while slowly rotating in his desk chair with a maniacal cat in his lap. "I don't hate you; I nothing you. You're like a beauty school mannequin head on which I get to show off some new toys and display my skills."

The doctor and I began our journey to redefine what was possible with the human body, and what was possible was getting rid of it.

One year I got x-ray, night vision eyeballs. I promised not to use both at once—I was allowed to spy on people changing, but only during the day. Other than that, the process was slow. One year I had to replace my kidneys and another year, my liver, due to the excessive amounts of drugs and alcohol I consumed. Eventually, I replaced all my organs, I had so many. I replaced my gallbladder with a mechanical one only to have it removed the following year; it turns out a mechanical gallbladder is an entirely useless fake organ.

As the years passed, I transformed into the being I am now. And plot twist alert, the doctor ended up becoming my best friend—no, that's a lie. I hated the guy all the way to the bitter end. I hope he gets eaten by land-piranhas—I truly do.

I was a different person than I once was. The only people still in my life from the start of this whole journey were the doctor and Germ. Germ and I weren't best friends like we used to be—his new life as a father and husband suited him well—but we still got together for the occasional drink. And honestly, I can't say that I looked any worse with my redesigned exterior than Germ did in his old age. You know who doesn't go gray? Robots. Everyone gets older, and everyone changes for the worse. This was just me embracing my true purpose.

I continued to replace every part of my body until there was nothing organic left to swap out. But it was an undeniable fact, I was a global icon, and everybody knew my name.

Chapter 18
The Beginning Part II

"Are you ready, Sir?" a woman dressed in baby blue scrubs asked, as I lay on the operating room table. I looked at her with dread in my eyes, I wonder if people could still read my expressions.

I took one last look at the crowd gathered in the stadium-like seats surrounding the operating table. Rodeos and space launches. I doubted any of the faces I saw would be of people that had passed through my life, but I still looked. None of the faces made any impression on me. I knew nothing about these people, yet they were going to see me in my last moments. I then noticed a young woman who reminded me of Sam. She was looking at her phone with barely a thought to my procedure.

There is an old philosophical quandary I had given much thought to. If while on a sea voyage, every plank on a ship is replaced one at a time until none of the original pieces remain, is it the same ship that returns to port? My answer is yes. Of course, I'm still the same ship because of my brain and because of my memories. But I guess we're almost to the "present," and I should try to explain why I've chosen to replace the last plank of wood on my body.

After many, many years of fame and identifying as part human and part mechanical sex robot, I decided to download my consciousness and my memories into a computer. The computer will replace the last piece of the original me, my brain. It is kind of like when your grandparents burned all of their VHS home movies onto DVDs, or like when your parents put all the DVDs onto hard drives as digital files, or like when your friends converted all those digital files into encoded water droplets.

Metaphors aside, this wasn't an impulsive decision. This was a decision grown from all my experiences since the day I was born. I spent most of my formative years with a single fear weighing on me. My most constant motivating factor as a child was a need to be different. There was a fear of not being special and realizing I was just like everyone else. So, life went on, and my uniqueness was validated, which only deepened the fear. I'm not qualified to psychoanalyze myself and determine why I had this phobia of ordinary. Let's just chalk this up to "it was probably my parent's fault" and move on—it's always the parents. Nothing frightened me more than the thought of waking up in fifty years, talking to my neighbor about how much I hated my wife and loved my lawnmower. Society was pushing me into a job I would end up dedicating way too much time to, which would also make me terribly unhappy. This is where I was headed before my accident. Getting hit by that truck was a goddamn miracle. It derailed my life and set me down a path no one had ever walked. I was special; I was unique; I was admired. But something happens when you finally elevate yourself above everyone else: you start to worry about falling back down.

Another source of anxiety I faced—which I share with just about everyone else in the world—was the fear of death. For some, this is paralyzing; it's so powerful it prevents you from living. If that's not irony, then I give up. Fear of death, in its essence, is a fear of not living enough. And as we discussed earlier, a fear of living was my issue. The premise was simple, if I could live a substantial life, then the memory of me could live on forever. Every action I took, whether I knew it or not, was working to make this dream a reality. All praise soothed my anxiety, if only slightly, and all moments of failure left me with dread.

I'm not sure if the expectations I had burdened myself with were fair. Being remembered forever is almost impossible. I defy you to think of more than a handful of people who will propagate through time. You might think George Washington was triumphant, and he will be remembered forever, but that's only true if America doesn't fall like many great civilizations before them. Our history is dependent on existing. Possibly a genius like Da Vinci or Einstein might have a shot? Well, those guys seem smart now, but people just naturally get smarter. If you adjust for inflation, they were unimpressive. In another hundred years, Einstein will be equivalent to a local news meteorologist. Jesus and Mohammed did an excellent job of solidifying their legacies, and at the very least, they will be a footnote in whatever future new religion infects this world. But again, for any mortal man, remembrance is predicated on the human race persisting through time. This is anything but a certainty. I think I've proved the next logical step in evolution has already occurred. Just like the original tenants on this planet, humans are on their way out.

I realize how convoluted this all sounds, but that's why people fear death—there's a lot of heavy stuff associated with it.

What does replacing my brain have to do with any of this? The mind is a muscle like any other part of the body. And it stands to reason, it will eventually fail me, and I will be left as nothing more than an expensive paperweight—people don't even use paper anymore. I realize replacing my brain may not be the safest decision; there is no guarantee as to what state this final surgery will leave me. Maybe who I am after the procedure will be congruous to death. Perhaps things will go perfectly, and there will be no change in my mental capacities.

I am not aiming for everlasting life. The only way to truly live forever is to never be forgotten. And the only way to be remembered forever is to never die. No need to reread my explanation; it was painfully circular.

Some people try to live forever through art, through achievement, through legacy, and all of these will work to some degree if you make enough of an impression. But my achievement, my legacy, is me; it's my existence. I will need to continually remind people I am alive—they won't be able to forget me if I don't die. People may read this book in 1000 years, not because it's a great book, but because they'll want to learn about the guy who cheated death. They may not understand one reference I make, but they will know who I am. They will pretend they know who I have been referencing and laugh, so they don't seem stupid.

When I fully integrate myself, I will achieve immortality. Regardless of whether or not I am aware of it, I will exist. People will not know the difference between me as a fully sentient humanoid or if I go full-robot, devoid of free will. To them, I will just be the same robot they've always known. This was it. This was the answer.

Again, I ask, "is it the same boat that arrives back into port?" The answer is the villagers waiting on the dock won't know the difference, so it doesn't really matter.

My eyes still laid on the girl in the crowd who reminded me of my lost love. Would this stranger remember me in 10 years, in 5 years or even a month from now? I had to remind myself it wasn't about her. Maybe she would forget, but someone would remember. Maybe her kids will see me in a commercial in 20 years or giving a speech at the U.N., or perhaps they'll see me in a PSA with the message to treat your robot servants better. Someone will remember.

"Yeah," I looked back to the nurse, "I'm ready." They were able to put me under so I wouldn't have to be awake for any of this. I imagine they were just putting me into power saver mode and dimming my functions. Either way, it had a similar effect to when I got my wisdom teeth pulled.

I began to count back from 10. "10...9..." If I could go back and change what happened to me, would I? What a silly question. You can't change the past. "...8...7..." I wish I were kinder to Sam. She deserved kindness. "...6...5..." I wish she were here. She would tell me she loved me and would always remember me. "...4..." I don't want to die. "...3..." And then I locked eyes with the girl who was on the phone. She was looking at me now, and I projected all my feelings onto her. This isn't the end for me, the world will remember. Anyways, all meaningful parts of my humanity died long before today. "...2..." The girl smiled, and a calm washed over me. "..."

The End

Author's Note

Thank you for reading my book. I am grateful to every single person who has took the time to read something I wrote. Being a self-published author, the burden of promotion and sales falls completely on my shoulders. Which is why I ask you to rate and review Superficial Intelligence on Amazon. If you liked this book, this is the most helpful thing you could do to support it.

5-Stars and a kind review never hurt anyone.

Also, if you enjoyed my writing, I welcome you to follow/subscribe to me on my website (comedicramblings.com) to read my existing work or get notification when I release new content.

Thank you,

Gregory Alesso

Made in the USA
Las Vegas, NV
16 December 2023